GEESE TO GHOSTS

A diverse collection of short stories

by

S.F. Formi and P.C.R. Penfold

Find P.C.R. Penfold on Facebook

Or email at: pcrpenfold@gmail.com

Contents

NOT DUNKIRK   by S.F. Formi

I hadn't thought of those days for years and then that young chap from the local rag came round. He wanted to know about Dunkirk; it was some sort of anniversary or whatever, wanted the personal angle from a survivor. But it was when he made that comment that I got a bit riled.

'Dunkirk must have been the most dramatic and exciting time of your life.'

'What makes you say that?' I said, after all he didn't know me.

'Well, Harry, you were just an ordinary kid from the East End, weren't you?' And then he said something about the rest of my life must have been 'humdrum' in comparison.

So I said, 'Well if you call riding the Wall of Death humdrum, then yes I suppose you're right.'

Of course, he didn't know what I was talking about so I rummaged about a bit and found some old snaps, tiny black and white pictures. He held them by their crinkled edges, yellow and brown with the years.

'What am I looking at?' he said, 'what's that?' His fingernail, none too clean, jabbed at the picture. Like so many today, this young fella didn't seem to see the need to pay any attention to his appearance – personal grooming they say these days, but there wasn't any in his case: rolled shirtsleeves, crumpled tie hanging out of a trouser pocket, jeans they were really. No jacket of course, hair curling over his collar and what they call designer stubble, I think. I sighed and turned back to the photos. I explained that he was looking at the Wall which was just a giant drum about 20ft high with narrow wooden boards running round the inside.

'And this,' he said, 'this bike, motorbike, you didn't ride that, on the Wall, did you?'

'I did,' I said, and told him about how you had to get the speed right or else it could be curtains. Jake, that was his name, seemed to have come to life. His eyes were huge as he studied the pictures and questions tumbled out: What was it like? How did I get into it? How did I train? Did anyone ever fall?

'Well now, young man,' I said, 'do you want me to talk about Dunkirk or the Wall of Death?'

It turned out, his appetite whetted; all he wanted to hear about was the madness of riding a motorbike up a wooden drum.

The words began to come, slowly at first, then it was as if I was reliving that time: the oil and petrol was in my throat; I could feel the throb of the engine between my thighs. I heard the raucous shouts of the crowd, egging us on. But I had to start at the beginning.

'You were right,' I said. 'I came from an ordinary East End family. It was a day trip to Southend with a mate that changed all that.'

I remembered that day, early June 1935. It came back to me as sharp and clear as ice: the smell of the ozone coming off the sea as Ted and I headed to the circus ground, then the people massing at the bottom of the huge drum.

'Blimey,' said Ted, 'did you see that?' It was the women's skirts ballooning in the air as they climbed the rickety steps to the viewing platform that had caught his attention. Ted nudged me. 'Get an eyeful of that.'

But I was too embarrassed and turned away from the sight of so many knickers and stocking tops, their owners shrieking in feigned alarm at the loss of their dignity.

'Let's get to the top quick,' I said. 'I want to see the start.'

Suddenly we were there, on the parapet, looking down at a man in leather trousers, his face glowing, and streaked with grease as he fired up his machine. Ted was saying something but the noise deafened any speech: a cacophony of engine roar, shouts and laughter, plus bellowed instructions from the management to move along, or not to lean over the parapet, PLEASE; all reverberating round the walls. An intense vibration began, causing a twitching in my legs and, perched as we were some twenty or so feet up, the whole thing was totally unnerving. I looked at Ted; he was grinning like a clown, and then the biker opened the throttle and I was gripped. Slowly at first then faster and faster he began the ascent, anti-clockwise, round the drum. I was mesmerised by the skill and daring as gradually he came close to the top, the colourful scarf he wore round his neck trailing in the draught like a flag of victory. Though strictly prohibited, there were women leaning over to touch and stroke his hair. For a second I thought he would come over the parapet; my fists clenched, but it didn't happen. My mouth fell open, as at one point, he raised an arm in salute to the crowd, controlling his machine with one hand. Gasps and screams greeted this feat.

I felt as if I had entered another world: one where anything was possible. I saw this man, this being, goad his machine with a twitch of his wrist, higher and higher; all around was the heavy, suffocating stench of oil, fumes, male and female sweat, mixed with the acrid smell of vinegar-drenched fish and chip papers. It engulfed me, took me over. I glanced at Ted: his rigid stance, his eyes wide with an amazed delight.

On the way home Ted and I talked incessantly. It was as if we had discovered something utterly strange and exciting. I could still taste the fish and chips, mixed in with all the other fumes and the unremitting din was in my ears. I tried to describe it to my parents.

'You've never seen anything like it.' I said to Mum's back as she cut up tomatoes and put them on a plate with bread and cheese for tea. 'That man,' I continued, 'dunno how he does it – keeps the bike from going over.'

From that day my life changed. I was working as a mechanic at the time and that stood me in good stead when I started trying to get involved. Every weekend following that first trip I went back to the circus and just watched. Each time the thrill was as intense as the first time. But there were lots of lads like me trying to get in on the act; some of them thought there was big money in it and others, like me, were just obsessed with the challenge of doing something so extraordinary.

'You have to remember,' I said to Jake, 'life in the 1930s was pretty drab. Working class boys like me had few opportunities for adventure. Most of us worked long hours, sometimes on apprenticeships lasting years, and on low wages, a good proportion of which would go to our mothers for housekeeping. In our spare time we might be kicking a ball around with our mates, having a pint in the local, not much more than that.'

So I was one of a number hanging around, asking questions, pestering the riders, running errands. But I was persistent and when the boss knew I had experience with engines, he gave me things to do: cleaning polishing and greasing. Eventually the riders accepted me, took me under their wing. Then came the great day when I was allowed to get on a bike, not to ride the Wall, not at first: I had to demonstrate that I could handle the machine. Well, that didn't take me long but when they let me try the Wall, I got a bit too excited and as I approached the ramp to begin the ascent my speed was all wrong; the bike flipped over and fell on top of me. It was a disaster, or so I thought at the time. I wasn't hurt, at least not physically, just my pride.

'It didn't put you off though?' said Jake.

'No. In fact it was the best thing that could have happened. I wasn't allowed to try again for a while, when the opportunity came I was careful: I knew what could happen and I wasn't going to mess up this time. The thrill of that ride! I will never forget it. But my first performance in front of an audience was electrifying. It felt like the bike had become part of me: the bike and me: me and the bike, my hand on the throttle, fumes, noise, the vibration through my body, the crowd in my head.

'And when I descended, the roar from the crowd filled the drum. I remember I stood there, head thrown back, arms spread, revelling in the tributes, shouts, whistles, catcalls. I drank it all in. Some people threw money on the ground. But I wasn't in it for the cash. And it seemed the audience liked me; I was a young fresh-faced chap and I suppose at the time, reasonably good-looking. Eventually I got a regular slot on the Wall and I gave up my day job.'

'What did your parents think of that?' said Jake.

I told him that it didn't go down well with the family. My parents were dead set against a life in the circus. To them, circus folk were not much better than gypsies, who at the time had a pretty bad reputation. Of course my mother worried that I'd injure myself and urged me to give it all up. It was no use and by then Louella had come on the scene.

Who was Louella, you ask? She was the most exotic creature I'd ever come across – nothing like the girls I'd known before. She was a trapeze artist and I could never get enough of watching her swing gracefully from one side of the Big Top to the other, her long legs flashing through the air, sequins glittering on her costume. She was a sight to behold I can tell you. She had long black hair and eyes almost as dark. If she thought you a fool those eyes would spark contempt and she'd toss her hair and walk away. I saw a lot of that! I was too young, too inexperienced for her tastes. She didn't want to know, not until that is, Suki came along.

'Hang on,' said young Jake at this point. 'First Louella, now Suki. What's going on?'

I laughed, 'No, you've got it wrong. Suki was a lioness.'

'What!' said Jake. 'You're having me on.'

'No,' I said, 'in fact I wasn't the only rider to make use of lions. For some of us it became an important part of the act – another draw. I got Suki as a cub and trained her to sit in the sidecar of the motorbike. She almost became like a member of the family, she was that tame. Of course nowadays people might say it was cruel or something: forcing an animal to spin round and round at high speed, but I really think Suki enjoyed it. I suppose she didn't know anything else. As she grew into an adult I had to be a bit more careful. We had to take precautions to make sure that she couldn't reach either me or anyone else, should the mood take her. Some blokes I knew carried guns, just in case. It wasn't something I ever considered.

'But I'm getting ahead of myself. I mentioned Suki because it was when she arrived that Louella first showed any interest in me. I think Louella liked the added edge of danger and daring that Suki brought into the picture. It gave me something extra. At least that's how it seemed and in no time, we were in the middle of a passionate romance.'

'Was Louella her real name?' Jake asked.

'Well,' I said, 'that's something I never found out, though of course I should have noticed when we signed the register.'

'Signed the register?'

'Yes, we got married. A quiet affair, just a couple of witnesses from the circus. My family didn't attend. They didn't approve.'

I thought back to the day I'd persuaded Louella to come home and meet Mum. Never again, you'd have thought there were icicles in the room, the atmosphere was that frozen. Dad excused himself and slipped away while Mum looked Louella up and down, her lip curling. Louella, of course, had refused to make any alterations to her style of dress, low neck, split skirt and much too much make-up for my family, so it wasn't really surprising that they didn't hit it off. But none of that mattered at all to me at the time of the wedding.

'We were married a few years,' I continued. 'Life was pretty hectic. Louella was always in demand, always surrounded by men. I didn't take a lot of notice in the beginning; I was too busy myself. The Wall was always popular and by this time I had a good reputation for delivering plenty of thrills in my act – Suki being a good part of it. But then the war hove into view and I was called up.

'After training I got embarkation leave and at the end when it was time to part, Louella was surprisingly emotional. She was a passionate woman, but never sentimental, so the softening I saw in her as we said goodbye was something new. I never saw her again,

As time went on and the letters from her dried up I realised I'd probably lost her. Trying to hold onto someone like Louella was like trying to pin a butterfly down. It took time, but after the war, with the help of my commanding officer, a divorce was arranged – all done through solicitors and letters. And then five years later I met Jean. We were married for thirty years.'

I looked up at Jake. He seemed to be a different person now, absorbed and engaged in what I'd been saying.

'That's quite a story Harry. I'm sure my editor will be interested. I may need to get back to you on a few things. Maybe get a photo or two. Is that all right?'

'Fine,' I nodded.

He gathered up his things, tape recorder and mobile phone, shook my hand and left.

After he'd gone, I couldn't help going back to those years. I thought about Louella and how it had felt: the fierce passion we'd shared. It had all been part of that other life, the circus, a world aside from ordinary living. A small world where people had to perform day after day to demanding audiences, always immaculately presented, always the wide smile, but outside the Big Top tempers often flared, relationships were broken, re-formed, broken again.

My marriage to Jean, by contrast, had been very different: sober, unexciting, predictable. She'd been a good wife, I suppose, but I'd always felt that there was something missing. To be honest, probably quite a lot was lacking in our relationship – for one thing I'd always wanted children. Jean didn't, and we didn't have any. I shrugged these memories away. So I was on my own now. It wasn't that bad. After all, I'd probably had more thrills and experiences than most.

About a week after the interview with Jake, I get a call from him, asking can he come round again. When he turns up he has a woman with him; Louise, he says her name is. It seems she's read the article on the Wall of Death and been intrigued. I look at her. She is about forty, dark hair bobbed just above the shoulders, a heart-shaped face – a look I'd always found very attractive. But I am puzzled. What can she want?

'You see,' she says, 'my grandmother's name was Louella. It's a bit unusual isn't it?'

'Well, yes,' I say, still baffled. I turn to Jake. His face is alight, attentive. He is perched on the edge of his seat as if waiting to burst in.

'Is there something else,' I say.

Jake shifts forward. 'Harry,' he begins, 'Louise's grandmother used to work in a circus, in Southend.'

I stare at him, then at her. 'Do you mean...' I say, 'do you mean you think she might be my Louella?'

They both nod. 'It's possible, yes,' says Jake.

'I've got a picture, not very clear but...' Louise produces a tiny photo, just like the ones I'd shown Jake before.

There is a young woman posing for the camera, her feet elegantly crossed in front, one hand resting lightly on the trapeze swing. Her hair is caught on top in a spangled net, one long black strand falling over her shoulder. She is wearing her circus costume and though the picture is black and white, I see in my mind the brilliant blues and reds that had once been so familiar.

I am stunned and my eyes blur with water as I remember.

But there is more. Louise starts speaking, but carefully as if her words might break something. She tells me her mother has been looking for me for years. But why? I ask.

Then comes the shocker: Louise's mother believes I am her father.

'No,' I say loudly. 'I never had any children.' I stop. They are both looking at me as if they know something I don't. Louise finishes the story. Louella had brought up her child alone, but when as a young adult her daughter started asking about her father, Louella named me. I said I reckon it was the easiest thing to say, and after all, we had been married at one time. It was all nonsense of course.

15

I tell them – I'd been away fighting, for years, and she hadn't been pregnant when I left. But as I speak a sudden memory strikes me, of Louella white-faced and blotchy with tears as we'd said goodbye that time. It wasn't like Louella, but surely that didn't mean... I would have known.

'When was your mother born?' I ask, my voice rough. Then I do some maths. I take a deep breath. It's just possible. I look at Louise: this is Louella's granddaughter. Then it hits me – this could be my granddaughter too.

'If you wanted to be sure,' says Jake, 'you could always have a DNA test.'

Do I want that, I wonder? My mind is whirling: one minute denying and the next thinking, maybe it's true.

'You say your mother's been looking for me?'

'Yes, for quite a while.'

What does it matter, I think. That woman needs to know her father, and as for Louise, she is looking like she's won the lottery, her hand up to her mouth, her eyes fixed on my face.

'What's your mother's name?' I ask.

'Harriett,' comes the reply.

BENNIE'S SECRET LIFE   by S.F. Formi

Bennie stretched and yawned; tiny daggers of teeth flashed briefly into   sight, ears twitching. For the moment, he seemed sunk in a deep reverie, but then he arched his back, gave another stretch, and jumped lightly from the chair to the floor. He stopped, head cocked, to listen to the house but all was still, apart from a low noise coming from upstairs. 'Snoring' he believed it was called. His whiskers drooped with disdain: but then, something about the regularity of the sound sent the blood pulsing through his veins.

A shiver went through his body. It was a call he couldn't resist. The time had come. He headed for the cat flap. It opened with a flick of a paw. They had forgotten to lock it, as usual. Leaving the house, he padded through the garden; the cool fresh scent rising from the damp grass tickled his nostrils and made him sneeze. He shook himself and squeezed under the fence, making his way through the field to the barn at the end. Unused and unloved, it was now the home of bats and owls, nesting swallows in summer and all manner of other small creatures, most of whom made a hasty exit at Bennie's approach. Bennie sat for a moment with his tail curled around his body – a neat figure on the dusty floor.

A sliver of pink appeared as he groomed a tuft of fur into its proper place. Satisfied with his efforts, he then gathered himself together and launched onto a large log. Once settled and comfortable he opened his mouth and let out a high-pitched yowl. Almost immediately there were rustlings from all corners of the barn; shadows slipped through the door. From a hole in the wood, Bennie clawed out an old metal object. He spent a few minutes cleaning off the dirt, after which some dulled and scratched red and gold colouring showed through, and it was possible to see the serpentine shape.

Then he raised himself on his hind legs, exposing a plump white belly as he grasped the neck of the instrument in one paw. With the other paw he began a light strumming on the ancient strings. The sound drifted around the barn calling forth other cats from the dark recesses and generating a mood of excitement. A large tabby began a soft humming in time to the music; a blue and white Siamese slid into some graceful ballet moves. By contrast, several old battle-bruised toms made their protest known.

'Pick it up Bennie,' they cried.

Bennie favoured them with a cold stare before continuing to play as before. His green/gold eyes then began following the lithe movements of a striking Persian cat. She sashayed up to Bennie and flicked his cheek with her dainty paw. Bennie hit a wrong note.

'Let's rock and roll baby,' she purred.

Bennie changed tack and a heavy beat exploded from the old rusting guitar, hitting the beams and echoing round the rafters. From nowhere, two feral cats appeared, one with a small drum and the other with a miniature keyboard.

In a moment the barn was alive with, 'Rockin' all over the World'; cats were jigging and jiving with the tabbies performing their most elaborate moves, puffing and panting as they went. The Persian sizzled and slithered between couples and groups: a nip here, a pat there.

The other inhabitants had had enough. There was a flapping of wings, a great cawing of rooks, as birds, owls and others departed. As the music died away Bennie caught sight of a stray creature left behind in the rush to leave the venue. Putting aside his guitar, he licked his lips before readying his body for action and pounced! The bones of the field mouse made a satisfying crunch as they met Bennie's teeth, the blood trickling down his throat, a warming and soothing accompaniment.

He gave himself a quick wash, yawned; his soft bed was calling. But one cat remained. The Persian was grooming her exotic fur, the silver coat falling in neat layers under her busy tongue. She looked up at Bennie, the golden eyes seeming to pierce through him. It was too much: Bennie gulped, shook himself and then padded over to her with firm steps. She rubbed her head under his chin, purring softly. 'I know a place...' murmured Bennie.

SEA CHILD   by P.C.R. Penfold

When Olivia saw the baby, she screamed. No one heard her and the sound settled around her like broken glass. She lay still for moments that flowed on and on. Slowly, and with a deadening certainty, she lifted her legs from around the still form. She saw the flutter of its pulse on the fontanelle, but it made no cry. Its face was so ugly and malformed the sight made her shudder and repress a second scream.

She struggled to the basin and washed herself and looked for a towel, then used it to wrap around the baby, suppressing her revulsion. Its eyes were still closed and for this she was grateful. She did not want to be judged, even by one so tiny.

She sat on the edge of the bed and pulled on shoes and then a coat. She picked up the still silent bundle and walked from the shack, down the treacherous cliff path and onto the beach. She was already tired and her footsteps dragged, leaving wraith-like trails in the sand. When she reached the cave, it was cool, damp, and deep, just as she remembered it from a long time ago. It was already steeped in tales of horror and was feared by many for being the home of a sea monster.

She stumbled across the glistening floor, having to use one hand to steady herself from slipping on the loose stones as the level dropped deeper and deeper. Her mind was devoid of emotion, all spent in that first scream. She had a purpose now.

The man who had fathered the child was at sea; the same sea which now roared in anger, throwing spray high into the grey air, settling with a crash onto the sand. He did not know he was a father. He would never know.

Olivia looked around. The cave mouth was like an ugly wound behind her; rarely lit by the sun: a place where life might spew from, rejected, like vomit. She shuddered. There were natural layers of rock, with crevices and shelves next to her, stretching back and lit by a small hole above her head where daylight looked down; a single eye that watched her every move. She placed the baby, not ungently, onto a shelf close to her head, and pushed it so that it stayed there.

Still it made no sound. She turned and retraced her steps, fumbling and floundering in her haste to leave.

The eye of the cave grew brighter and the warm air caused droplets that had clung to the rock face to fall. The baby opened her eyes. Water trickled straight into her mouth. Eagerly, she sucked as more slid onto her tongue. She was not alone. Above, bats circled, coming home to roost before dawn broke, with steely shards of light. Spiders scurried, leaving trailing webs: scaffolding from rock to rock; and lower down, lizards slithered and skittered. The cave was alive with these muted sounds: moisture dripping, and air being wafted by paper-thin wings.

There was also a youth named Adam, hiding in the cave. He, despite very poor eyesight, had watched everything. He felt pity for the abandoned baby; he too, had been rejected by his father: scolded and punished for being unable to do the chores set him, because he could not see sufficiently well. His father was a carpenter, and a son with such poor eyesight was of no use to him. Adam had not been abandoned physically like the baby, but at the age of twelve he had chosen to leave, and now he lived here in this dark cave, hidden away from a world which he felt he could never be part of.

When the woman was far away, Adam went over to where the baby lay and pulled back the blanket. He could feel that her eyes were not properly aligned, and that her nose and mouth were conjoined. Her eyes were open and her limbs jiggled at his touch and that made him smile. He took the corner of her blanket and dipped it in a puddle

21

and squeezed it into her open mouth. She seemed to stretch out to him for more and grabbed his finger in a vice-like grip. It made him laugh, all that strength in one so tiny.

The baby survived and it had to be a miracle. Adam crushed fish and seaweed and mixed it with the water that formed in the cave and fed it to her. He lifted her out from the shelf and took her to the sea where he washed her. He laid her body on his while he floated and she seemed to like it, arms and legs thrashing. He did this several times a day to keep her clean. He continued to feed her with fortified water and against all the odds, she continued to thrive.

He named her Eve, (because he was Adam) and he taught her how to play in the sand as well as swim in the sea. When the weather turned cooler, although it was never cold, they stayed within the cave where the temperature was constant. He used the blanket to clothe her but knew that he must find more for her to wear. He sang to her and she copied his voice, his movements and learned the words. She scrambled over the rocks in the cave like a monkey and learned to walk. He worried when she scurried off into the sea ahead of him, but she had learnt to swim before she could walk.

No one came, not the woman nor anyone else. He hoped she would never return. This was his haven. Day by day and year by year, they played and talked, swam, and ate raw seaweed, fish and molluscs. They ate other foods too, if Adam ventured beyond the cliff to where there were fruit trees. He also went as far as the markets sometimes and stole bread and picked up food from the ground, but those were anxious times, when he might lose his landmarks for directions to return and he worried all the time he was away, about Eve hurting herself or drowning.

When he was teaching her to swim, he would tie his wrist to hers, using seaweed. If he left her to go foraging, he would tie her wrist to a rock inside the cave, but one day, she learned how to eat through it and free herself. She tried to follow him but tired before she reached the cliff. She did this many times and Adam did not stop her.

One day at the market, Adam watched a music man playing a mouth organ. The man seemed to have two heads, but then the second head revealed itself as a monkey which had been sitting on his shoulder. The monkey took off its little hat and moved into the crowds, expecting coins to be thrown into it. When the monkey stopped in front of Adam, he shook his head. He had no money. The monkey delved into the hat and offered him a coin instead. Everyone applauded and the music man nodded his head. Adam found he had enough money to buy two smocks. They were all the same size: one for himself and one for Eve.

Eve wanted to know all about his trips and of course, again she wanted to go with him. He said it wouldn't be the same if she were there. He tried to explain: his father had known he would be a burden, but usually, as children grow older and bigger, they became independent and helped with the chores until one day, the roles would be reversed and the child would look after the parent. He told her that his father only saw him as a millstone, never reaching independence and this had made his father angry and he had punished Adam.

He went on to explain that when he went to the market, people did not have to take responsibility for him and so they weren't angry like his father had been. Instead, they felt pity and that made them generous. If they saw two burdens, he said to Eve, they might feel only resentment. He knew this wasn't quite the truth nor was it quite what he meant, but he knew in his heart that she would not invoke the same pity as his lack of sight did. He did not think of her as ugly, but he also knew she was not like the young children he saw there. She was short: much too short for her age. Her head was large and her features unbalanced. He would spare her the prejudice of not being like others if he could. These were the things he didn't say.

His explanation did not stop Eve from wanting to leave. So far, the climb up the cliff had proved too much for her short legs, and it

23

must have been eight summers before she decided to defy him. Before the dawn was brightening the sky, and even though Adam heard her leave, she went out and Adam did not stop her. It took her many hours to climb the cliff and when she finally found the marketplace, she was tired and anxious. The crowds and the noise terrified her. People stared and pointed at her; mothers pulled their children away from her. She had only ever observed kindness in Adam's face, or laughter, and sometime sadness: what she saw in the faces of these strangers was none of these, and she recognised it as fear and revulsion. She fled back to Adam and safety, sobbing all the way.

Adam said nothing; he could not comfort her with lies, but he resolved to make life better for them both, as he could see now that they were bound together forever. When he had left his father's home, he had brought with him a blanket, an extra smock, shoes he seldom wore, a knife and a wooden comb his father had made for him. But he had an ambition which was to make fire and cook. He now felt that if the cave was to be their permanent home, it should have fire. He already had a pot and other vessels which had washed up on the shore, and there was plenty of driftwood. Crabs and lobsters were unpleasant eaten raw and he had never touched the raw meat that was occasionally available. Their diet would be greatly improved if he could cook this food. He decided he would whittle some pegs to sell at the market and with the money he saved, he would buy a tinder box. Eve was very impressed; Adam had never shown such determination before. She told him he was very clever and waited for the great day when their home would be so much improved.

People came to recognise the partially sighted youth from the market and knew that he lived in the cave and made smoke. From far away on the cliff top, they spotted him frolicking out at sea, apparently playing with what they assumed was a seal. Both looked so elegant in the water and stories grew up about his relationship with the seal. They were always together. They would lie on the

24

rocks and the seal, which was of course, Eve, would squirm around on her belly before they disappeared from view into the cave.

They thrived and lived on for many years, until one day a great storm rattled buildings, flinging roofs into the sky and twisting trees, sending them sprawling across the countryside. The cave was flooded, and its opening became an underwater prison and the two occupants, terrified, climbed higher and higher, until there was nowhere else to go.

No one knew whether the pair had been carried out to sea or drowned in their cots, but they were never seen again, nor were they greatly missed. Adam's father had put aside the memory of his son and never knew that he had become strong and independent, reliant on nobody. The woman, Olivia, never knew that her daughter Eve, was the seal people talked about, who had gambolled so gracefully in the sea with Adam. Despite remaining unloved except by each other, their story slipped quietly into legend.

THE GOSSIPS   by P.C.R. Penfold

Miranda looked around the café with a sense of achievement. The members of a local art studio had hung some of their pictures which were for sale, and these had given the walls a splash of colour and contrast with the pale grey tablecloths and pale pink napkins. She had also set up a bookcase for people to bring and exchange books, hoping that they would stop and read while drinking coffee. She wanted to promote a feeling of leisure and a café with people in it was so much more inviting than an empty one. Maybe then her customers would choose savoury snacks and stay for lunch as well as cakes.

The doorbell clanged and Miranda gave her first customers time to choose where to sit before she approached them. They were three women and they asked for hot chocolate and a plate of assorted cakes to choose from. After serving them, Miranda put on some classical music, quiet and gentle and not intrusive. She asked them after a while, if they minded the music and they all looked relaxed, nodding their approval. The youngest of the three said it wasn't the sort of thing she normally listened to but she found it peaceful and atmospheric. Good, thought Miranda, just what I wanted. She retreated to her position behind the coffee machine to tidy up. Even so, she couldn't help overhearing their conversation.

'She said she wanted to murder him! I suppose it's just the way people
talk of course.

But then he was found dead, heart attack they said, but could you be sure?'

'I never did trust her, close set eyes and that awful dyed red hair.'

'That doesn't make her a murderer! Poor woman, you're maligning her!'

'Were there children?'

'I don't believe so. I feel sorry for her, the way people are gossiping just because they didn't get on.' This was from a gentler looking woman and said with an apologetic glance at Miranda.

'Well, it was more than that, I'd say: the rows in public, the shouting and doors slamming when you walked past the house. Although I'll admit it was mostly him you could hear.'

The doorbell chimed again and a shocked silence fell as the target of their gossip walked in with a young man. Miranda didn't know any of these people but she was in no doubt about the identity of her newest customer. The hair was sufficient to identify her, it was as red as a turkey's coxcomb. She wouldn't have agreed about the eyes though. They were more frightened looking than anything else. The couple came to the counter to make their choices.

The three women were unable to find anything else to talk about now and were looking at each other for inspiration with widened eyes. Miranda was so glad she had the music playing: it cut through the sudden silence. She ushered her customers to a seat by the window and said she would bring their order in a few minutes. She listened with amusement as the most critical of the three gossipers turned to the redhead saying how sorry she was for her loss. The redhead smiled shyly and thanked her, then introduced her companion.

'This is my brother, Mark. And I'm Ellie, but I expect you know that.'

The three women nodded and smiled sympathetically. It was several minutes before they could think of anything else to say to each other, aware now that they would be overheard. Miranda turned the music up; she couldn't have her first day spoiled by an uncomfortable atmosphere. She reminded herself that she couldn't choose her customers either. She decided some initiative was required. Having delivered the couple's order, she lingered at their table, asking them how well they knew the town as she was new to

27

it. Mark let Ellie do the talking; he said it was not his home, he was just visiting.

Ellie looked sad. 'I don't know many people. I used to be a fitness instructor so now, since my husband died, I'm hoping to get back into it. There's a leisure centre not far out of town. I think I'll try there.'

Miranda's smile was warmly encouraging. 'Good idea. I'd be interested in that. What do you say ladies?'

'Oh yes, great idea.' They all nodded in disingenuous agreement. Miranda moved back behind the counter and was pleased when the conversation continued without her aid, the women asking Ellie when she would start and if she would give classes or train people on the machines.

The doorbell clanged again and a young man came straight to the counter.

'Have you got something I can take away to eat?'

Perfect, thought Miranda, all that late night baking had not been in vain. 'Sausage rolls? Pasty? Veggie squares? I can heat it if you like or make you a sandwich? Anything you like.'

'Marvellous! Pasty please. In fact, I'll have two, heated up.' He looked around the café while Miranda put them in the oven. His face lit up.

'Hi Ellie! Glad to see you're getting out.' He walked over to Ellie and embraced her. The women nearly fell off their seats with curiosity but no explanation was forthcoming. He pulled up a chair while he was waiting for his pasties. 'Shall I come over later? Sort out the boiler? I had it all booked in, but you know, I didn't know if....' He tailed off, apparently too embarrassed to mention her bereavement.

'Yes please, I need it sorted out.' They both looked relieved and he stood up to collect his lunch from Miranda. 'Two o'clock all right?'

The women exchanged knowing looks. Perhaps Ellie was about to embark on an affair having polished off her husband. The three were floundering in their attempts to have a normal conversation.

The less critical one asked after the son of the oldest one. The woman ignored the question and again turned to Ellie.

'It's so important to have the boiler working isn't it dear? Is he a good mechanic, your young man?'

Ellie ignored the innuendo. 'He's very reliable, he services it regularly and I've never had any bother with it until this week. Things seem to keep going wrong, now that, well, you know, my husband's death.'

'How dreadful for you. What did he die of?' Her younger companion pressed her knee under the table and glared at her. It made no difference and the question sat between them waiting for an answer. Mark leaned across to his sister.

'It's all right Ellie, drink up and we'll go.' He turned to the group. 'I expect you mean well, but my sister isn't ready for all these questions from strangers.'

The youngest one quickly stood up.

'I'm Annie. I live three doors down from your house. Would you like to come for coffee one day? Say Thursday at 11am?' She knew she was gabbling but she felt ashamed of her friends. Ellie smiled and nodded. At that moment, Annie wasn't at all sure that Ellie would come but she hoped she would. She picked up her bag and turned to her friends.

'I have an appointment later and I need to go home and change first. Bye.' She went to the counter and paid, then walked through the door feeling a great weight leave her shoulders. She was well aware that she had arranged to see Ellie but had made no such agreement with her friends. Their cattiness had shocked her and all her sympathy was with the redhead and her sweet, shy smile.

Miranda was relieved when an elderly couple came in next. When they were settled, they smiled at the others in the café. Ellie and Mark were collecting shopping bags, but the two women were already talking about Annie. Then Ellie and Mark took their receipt to the counter and paid.

'Come again soon.'

Almost before they were clear of the door, Ellie grabbed hold of Mark's arm.

'Oh, that was awful. They know! I could tell. Did you see the way they were looking at me?'

'Don't be silly, of course they don't know. What is there to know anyway? Anyone would think you'd poisoned Bob. Pull yourself together Ellie, this won't do at all.'

Ellie giggled tearfully. 'No. I mean they know about me and Dave, the boiler man.'

Mark looked at her and began to laugh.

'Ellie, Bob was a complete and utter pig to you. He hit you, put you down in company, criticised everything you did. I'm glad if you've found someone who's nice to you, you deserve it. Never mind the neighbours, those women would find mice droppings in a cake mix, all except Annie that is. I think you may have found a new friend in that one.'

They linked arms and walked back home.

'I like the new café, by the way, don't you?'

FALLEN FROM GRACE   by S.F. Formi

'The Fall Occurs at Dawn': Albert Camus

Heels clip against the paving slabs, echoing in the silent city. A lone streetlamp sends a flare of light around her feet as she walks. One foot in front of the other, not far now. The sound of her own footsteps provokes a memory of lying in bed as a child, the house too cold to sleep and hearing the return of Anna next door: her beehived hair, siren red lips and nails to match. She'd thought Anna so glamorous, but that wasn't what her mother called her.

'Tart,' her mother spat the word whenever Anna, or a mention of her, came within her orbit. At the time Dotty hadn't understood it and didn't care anyway. Anna had nice clothes, even if her skirts were a bit on the tight side, her tops rather low. But then perhaps she'd been short on material. Dotty grinned at this memory; she'd assumed everyone made their own clothes in those days.

She sighed. It had been a hard week. It was no fun standing outside in the rain and if it hadn't been raining it was windy and cold, night after night. She'd had to squash into shop doorways or under awnings with the other girls. But it was over, for now, and tomorrow was her day off. A gust of wind pushed her sideways; puffing slightly she struggled to keep her balance. Her phone rang.

She reached inside her anorak and clamped the mobile to her ear.

'Hello Mum,'

'Dotty how are you? You haven't rung for ages now.'

'I'm fine Mum. Don't worry.'

'So is everything OK?'

'Yes of course. I'm just watching a bit of telly.'

'That's nice. Kids all right?'

'Yes, absolutely.'

'When are you bringing them to see me?'

'Soon, Mum, soon.'

'Dave OK? Still bringing in the money?'

Silence.

'Dotty?'

'Yes, yes of course.'

She put the phone away and walked up her garden path. Inside, the woman on the sofa stirred and sat up.

'Everything OK?' said Dotty.

'No problem,' said her neighbour.

Dotty got out her purse and handed over some cash.

Alone, she kicked off her shoes and poured a glass of whisky. Holding the glass to her nose she inhaled the smoky peatiness before putting it to her lips. The warmth of the room after the long cold night was soothing. She thought of her mother: such an upright woman, so high principled, a result of her strict religious upbringing. What would she say, if she knew?

But at least, thought Dotty, my children are well fed and warm. Her aching legs sank into the softness of the sofa. She took another sip from the glass.

OPPORTUNITY KNOCKS   by S.F. Formi

It looked abandoned, in the middle of the yard. But of course, it was not 'abandoned' in that sense of the word. The chauffeur and other servants would be inside the public house, taking their leisure. This being the case he indulged himself in a long inspection, noting the finer details of the vehicle. What would it feel like to drive a car like this? Would it start up immediately, he wondered.

He stroked his long face and pulled at his ears as he pondered his own question. This would be the type of vehicle that might win him the girl of his dreams; a girl who would forget about his deficiencies, of which there were many as he was well aware. His gaunt face was framed by two large ears and finished with round bulbous eyes and a sharp nose. His appearance, with the lean, lanky body had been variously described as 'weaselly,' 'like an overgrown elf', or the most insulting, just plain, 'creepy.'

But this was no time to indulge in self-pity, not that he was inclined to do that in any event. His own view was that, whilst he accepted that his features were somewhat less than traditionally deemed handsome, nevertheless, wasn't there something to be said for 'difference'?

Abandoning all such reflection, he determined to focus on the possibilities that lay before him: this machine, this beautiful machine, would surely enable a quick get-away, when the occasion arose? His mind wandered to that velvet-lined box, snugly sitting in the dowager's dressing room. Of course, he had never seen the jewels that resided within, but he had heard all about them. It was pure chance, or maybe it was fate, that had brought the dowager's nephew into his restaurant that night. The young man was already 'in his cups', as Egbert tended to put it. His condition increased his tendency to speak in a loud voice, allowing Egbert, in his comings and goings to the table, to pick up a great deal of useful information.

Egbert was convinced that, this time, everything would go according to plan. It may be that, in the past, similar ventures had not worked out quite as he'd wished. But this was different. Of that, he was sure.

These thoughts filtered through his mind as he worked his way stealthily around the car. He tried the driver's door. To his amazement, it swung open at his touch. How careless, how fortuitous! He clambered in; jamming his cap on his head at what he thought was a jaunty angle.

Soon, he was bowling along the country lanes, the motor responding to every touch. It was a dream drive. On reaching the ancient manor, he switched off the engine to study the building for a moment. It was important to know the entrances and exits, although of course he would not use them. The building stood, proud and dominant, part of the landscape as it had been for four hundred years. Ivy clung to its weathered façade, almost covering some of the windows; Tudor chimney pots stood as watch towers over the surrounding acres and, for a moment, Egbert faltered: he had never made an attempt on such an intimidating property. Even if the family were away from home, and he knew they were, there would be servants.

But Egbert knew his worth; self-doubt was not a failing with him and having tucked the car out of sight in some bushes, he crept up to the back of the house and, wrapping his bony limbs around a drainpipe, he commenced his climb. With his almost prehensile arms the ascent presented no problems. On reaching a convenient ledge he found a window left ajar; a little brute force rendered the opening wide enough for Egbert to slide his slim torso inside. He slipped to the floor and waited a moment to get his bearings. He was good at this; orienteering had been a passion of his as a boy.

He was in a corridor: it stretched ahead, seemingly for miles. It occurred to Egbert, rather late in the day, that he had no idea which of the many doors opening off this long walk might lead to the dowager's bedroom. He began to move along, peering into the rooms as he came to them. He reasoned that the dowager's one would be large and likely to be over-stuffed with furniture from another era. He had just arrived at this conclusion and was feeling very pleased with his deductions when a figure emerged from one of the rooms just ahead. Egbert started; he had not allowed for this. The figure approached. It was a young woman.

'Hallo,' she said, 'and who are you?' She seemed interested, rather than perturbed by his appearance. This gave Egbert the notion that she was one of the servants. Her apron and cap also helped with this suspicion.

With great presence of mind, Egbert swept the driving hat from his head and managing a half-bow, said 'Good day. I am so sorry to intrude upon you but I am looking for the dowager's room.'

'And what might you be wanting with that?' A smile flitted around her mouth and she looked at him from under her lashes as she spoke.

'I have come to repair something for her ladyship.' Edgar was thinking fast, something he often had trouble with. 'It's in her dressing room.'

'Oh,' she said, her expression changing, 'the drawer in her chest that sticks. I suppose it's that.'

Egbert nodded, 'Yes, exactly.'

She looked puzzled. 'But how did you get in? Mr Barnes is having his rest and the others are on a half day.'

'Yes, Mr Barnes did let me in. I did not wish to disturb his *siesta* so I assured him I could find my way.'

By now, Egbert was beginning to perspire, but the maid nodded and appeared satisfied.

'It's the third door on the right. Will you be all right, or do you need me...?'

'No, no, not at all. My thanks for your help.'

Egbert moved off, looking back over his shoulder to be sure she wasn't following him. Not the sharpest knife in the drawer. Was that the expression he'd heard recently?

35

Once inside the room, Egbert had no problem in locating the jewel box. The dressing room was off the bedroom and was unlocked, as was the chest containing the silver casket, exactly as described by the dowager's nephew. Egbert's scaly hands reached out for his prize and his eyes gleamed. There was disappointment when he discovered that though much else in this house was open to the world, this box was definitely not. He ground his teeth in exasperation but decided he would deal with that problem later.

He turned to leave the room, the box clutched close, when the door opened. She stood there, a triumphant grin on her face.

'Caught you, red-handed!'

'What, what do you mean?' Egbert was stammering. 'I was just about to...'

'I know what you were just about to do,' she said.

She seemed different to Egbert. Her face, which had appeared to him at first a bit loutish and almost blank, was now alive with a cunning, foxy look to it.

'I assure you...' he began

'But it's locked,' she said. 'The box. Not a problem, to me. I know where she keeps the key.' She nodded.

Egbert was bewildered. He had no idea what she intended him to understand by this.

'I could call the police.'

'The police? No, no. There's absolutely no need for that.'

'I agree. Not if we make a deal.'

The car sped along the road, the silver casket on the bench seat between Maisie and Egbert. She was thrilled with its red sportiness and had insisted on 'putting it through its paces.' Egbert sat; his eyes had the look of a hung-over bloodhound that had lost its sense of direction. How had it come to this? He was careering along in a stolen car, driven by a parlour maid. He braced himself against the dashboard, his stomach lurching, as she swung the vehicle around a sharp bend.

She gave him a quick glance. 'She won't miss the jewels for weeks. Aunt Griselda never wears them these days.' Her words sunk in, but slowly. A few moments passed, then,

'Aunt Griselda?' he said, his voice high and shaky.

'Surely you didn't take me for the maid?' Her laugh was not music to his ears. 'I was on my way to a fancy-dress party. Have you ever been to Nice?' she continued, 'I'm sure we will find an outlet for your talents there.' She patted his thigh. Egbert winced.

MY UNCLE FRED   by P.C.R. Penfold

Millie, my Labrador had been in next door's pond again and a wet dog smell rose from her coat. It was so much like the smell of my Uncle Fred's tweed jacket after a downpour, I almost had to look around to make sure he wasn't standing behind me. It set me to reminiscing – how the jacket emitted a dry smell as well, but that was different because it was pipe tobacco. The damp jacket smell did not have the same evocative power as the tobacco scent. The brand was Ogden's St Bruno Flake, and it came in a small oval shaped white tin with brown writing on the lid. I would watch with childish fascination as he stuffed the shreds of tobacco into the pipe, then tamped it all down with a special metal tool. To my young eyes this was very clever. The tool had several functions; another one included a curved blade to scrape the bowl of the pipe clean after use. Then would follow a search in his pockets for the special pipe lighter, which he would hold on its side so that the flame came through little holes and did not burn his fingers. The pipe filling and drawing to keep it alight was a ritual I loved and carefully observed.

When the solicitor phoned to tell my mother and me of Uncle Fred's death, I asked if I might be allowed to sort out my uncle's belongings. It felt the right thing to do and perhaps it would help to assuage my guilt for not having visited him for such a long time.

I visited the house the next day and as soon as I entered and put down my bag, my eyes were drawn to it. There it was: the tweed jacket I remembered so well, hanging on the back of the door, as shabby and smelly as ever. I was back in my childhood, standing in front of his seated figure with my hands on his knees as he sat and performed his predictable pipe lighting routine.

I had other memories of him, of course. He had an unruly mop of curly brown hair which never seemed to change in length, and a craggily lined face and warm brown eyes. He was kind and would answer all my childish questions with a joke. He was always playing tricks on me, retrieving a coin from behind my ear or hiding things in his hand which he had taken from my pocket. All that time ago, at the age of eight, I had adored him and now, guilty tears pricked my eyes, because neither my mother nor I had seen him for many months. We had drifted apart when she and I moved in with my mother's friend Brian. Then the teenage years had taken over my life.

I never stopped to wonder what he did when we weren't there. After the move and the change in our circumstances, our contact had been reduced to Christmas and birthdays: he always sent me lovely, thoughtful birthday presents whereas mine to him were often socks or tobacco. Now, as I opened drawers and delved into pockets, my findings belied the belief that he only had a life when my mother and I took the bus to pay him a visit. I realised that I had not taken the trouble to get to know him as an adult. Far too late, I was being given the chance to see into his life.

I sat at his little desk, where I found envelopes stuffed with bills and receipts, all neatly filed. There was one labelled 'sundry,' and this revealed train tickets, birthday cards I had sent him and old theatre programmes. I didn't know that Uncle Fred had liked the theatre. I put them on one side to show Mum. Then, at last, I picked up the tweed jacket that had held so many memories for me. I slipped it on, feeling its hairy roughness and realised that all these years later, it fitted me. I put my hands in the pockets and twirled about, laughing at myself. There was nothing in them, and I wondered if he had in fact stopped wearing it due to its extreme age. Then I checked an inside pocket. I found a piece of paper covered with pub names, phone numbers and dates. How odd, I thought and on impulse, and driven by curiosity, I phoned a couple of them, ostensibly to let them know of his death, but really, I wanted to find out why he had so many pub numbers. He had never struck me as a drinker or even one who might be interested in pubs at all.

After drawing a few blanks, and 'sorry, no, was he a regular then?' which I could not truthfully answer, I found someone who knew him.

'Old Fred's gone then, has he?' said the publican of The White Horse. 'He'll be sadly missed. He used to do a stand-up comedy piece every Thursday. Old jokes, but he had a way of telling them which had everyone in stitches. We paid him with a glass of whisky, plus a little cash whip round. Nice old boy.'

From the dates, I could see that he had entertained at some of the pubs quite recently. I wondered why he had never told us, could it have been pride? He clearly did not own very much. My heart clenched guiltily at the thought that he may have believed we would not be interested.

After that, I flipped through the theatre programmes, and there I found his name in very small print, listed as the audience warm-up entertainer during the intermission. It felt strange and sad, not ever knowing this side of my Uncle Fred. I tried to console myself that as a small child I had been his very appreciative audience of one, all those years ago. His wallet held a couple of £10 notes and a pawnbroker's ticket, proving that he had still been wearing the ancient jacket. I couldn't imagine what he might have pawned. I knew nothing of the working of those places, so I looked up the address and resolved to find out a little more.

The shop was packed with what looked to me like a lot of junk, except for a large display cabinet behind the counter. This held smaller items of higher value. The proprietor stood in front of it as if he were guarding it. The room had an atmosphere of forgotten people and sad memories, every piece having a story to tell, silenced by its journey's end into this drab place. Did many people come back to retrieve their precious bits and pieces, I wondered, no doubt at a considerable loss?

I held out my ticket to him, by way of introduction. He looked at me sharply or so I thought, his eyes assessing me, maybe trying to guess what I had come to collect, but perhaps that was more guilt on my part. After all, it wasn't my ticket that I was handing over. He checked the number against a neatly written column in a well-thumbed book, one long finger travelling swiftly before it stopped and jabbed the page.

'Mr Bright?' He asked rather sarcastically I thought, since I was clearly female.

'My Uncle,' I said, 'my father's brother; he died last week.' I showed him my driver's licence with my name, Amanda Bright. He nodded, then taking a key from his pocket, he unlocked the cabinet. His hand hovered briefly then came to rest on a handsome gold pocket watch. He named quite a large sum that he required for its redemption. He took the money and put a line through his book entry. After the business had been transacted with a slamming of the till drawer, he became more relaxed and willing to chat.

'I remember your uncle. He used to have this watch in and out more times than a rabbit down a hole. I have a lot of customers like that, but Fred came back more often than most.'

I walked back to my uncle's flat in reflective mood. Then an unhappy realisation struck me. All those lovely presents he used to send me every year on my birthday must have been the reason he pawned his beautiful Hunter watch. He would perform stand-up comedy in the pub to help pay back the pawnbroker and once again be able to retrieve his watch. I felt so sad; all those months I hadn't been to see him, yet he always thought of me and had been generous when he could ill afford to be. I hoped that he had enjoyed putting on his comedy turns and magic shows and the popularity he achieved was company for him. But one fact remained to remind me of my guilt.

In all those years, he had never bought himself a new tweed jacket.

AUNT LETITIA COMES TO TEA   by S.F. Formi

Kylie is leaving the house. She opens the front door and jumps back, startled to find a woman standing there, hand outstretched to ring the bell.

'Oh hi,' she mutters, 'just off.'

'Good afternoon, Kylie,' says the other.

'Yeah,' says Kylie, 'gotta go.'

'Go?' says Aunt Letitia, 'but I've come to see you. Didn't your mother mention it?'

'Yeah, well, don't remember.' Kylie chews her multi-coloured nails and tries to edge past Aunt Letitia, who puts out a hand to detain her.

'Kylie,' she says with a determined face, 'I have spent two hours on a dirty, crowded, train, forced to listen to other people's fatuous conversations. I would now appreciate the offer of some tea and company.'

Kylie looks up from under black-tarred eyelashes. 'What's fatuous?' she says.

Aunt Letitia tuts in exasperation and barges into the house. Kylie saunters behind her, dragging the too-long sleeves of her cardigan over her hands and attempting to pull the rest of the garment across her chest.

'You might well try to cover yourself, young lady,' says Letitia, looking for somewhere to sit amongst the beer cans and plates greasy with congealing leftovers. 'That top is far too revealing; it's quite shocking on a young girl like you.'

Kylie pouts and swings about a bit.

'Not only that – it's unhealthy. You'll catch your death in this weather.'

Kylie turns to her nails again and says nothing.

Aunt Letitia perches on the corner of a sofa, pushing the empty take-away cartons to one side.

'Well, where's your manners Kylie? Aren't you going to offer me something?'

Kylie mutters under her breath, then looks up and says, 'Doyouwannadrink then?'

'A cup of tea would be very nice, and some Rich Tea if you have any.'

'Only got ordinary tea – nothing special,' says Kylie, frowning.

Aunt Letitia sighs. 'Rich Tea is a biscuit, not a tea. It goes with a cup of tea.'

Kyle stomps off to the kitchen and returns in a few minutes with the drinks, teabags floating on top. Aunt Letitia looks at the muddy liquid in the builders' mugs. She has been taking in the disordered state of the house.

'Is your mother at work dear?'

'No, not now.'

'She's shopping, is she?'

Silence

'Kylie, are you going to tell me where your mother is?'

Kylie looks up, her face reddening and says nothing for a moment, then, 'why are you bothered anyway?

'I am concerned for you – of course I am. After all I am your godmother.' Aunt Letitia rearranges her gloves and handbag. Her mouth is a tight line against the tone of Kylie's outburst.

'My boyfriend is staying with me.' It's almost a whisper and Kylie keeps her head down.

'Boyfriend!' Aunt Letitia jerks up. There is a silence while she absorbs this information. Then, 'but your mother, where is she?

'Hospital,' says Kylie. 'She's had an operation.'

'Oh,' says Aunt Letitia. 'I didn't know. What is wrong? Nothing serious I hope.'

Kylie gulps and her lip trembles. 'She's got cancer.'

Aunt Letitia's mouth drops open. 'I'm so sorry,' she says, and again, 'I didn't know.'

'That's where I was going,' sniffs Kylie, 'to the hospital.'

Aunt Letitia gets up and goes over to Kylie, wrapping her lavender scented arms around the girl. 'We'll go together,' she says, 'and you know cancer is very treatable these days. I'm sure everything will be OK.'

Kylie turns her face into the bony shoulder; her mascaraed eyelashes now turned to black goo, leave a nasty mark on the cashmere coat.

AUTUMN

by P.C.R. Penfold

Leaves spiral and lift, obeying a silent command
    they quiver then settle
damp and still, to feed the earth.
Flowers fade and droop,
    retreating
 back to their roots.

Clouds, the colour of grapes, glow purple and gold
    in an eerie light.
A shaft of sunlight strikes a globe of rainwater
    winking,
then setting it ablaze.

Flocks of birds, serious and intent,
    gliding in unison,
    heading west.
Cats basking by fires,
    abandoning their summer haunts.
Autumn evenings of frost and ice
    longer nights and shorter days
    as patiently
Winter waits her turn.

SNIFFING THE AIR   by S.F. Formi

(first published on Platform for Prose 2019)

There was to be a policy meeting. It was a most unusual occurrence; there were frequent strategy meetings, other meetings to discuss the state of the larder, meetings to decide whether the birth rate was going up or down. Occasionally there would be extra-ordinary meetings, perhaps to make senior appointments or to confer over a new hazard or threat.

The wolves approached, singly or in pairs, padding into place and forming a circle of grey and white around the leader. Ajax watched as each wolf lay down in submission, tail twitching – just enough, no more. Alexia, his mate, sat on the raised mound they shared. Her body was as still and silent as the ice around her but her eyes darted here and there. If she chanced upon a restless cub the soft mouth would harden and her gaze would become steely. In terror the cub would try to disappear into his mother's coat.

When it seemed every wolf was in place, a hush fell over the group. Then Ajax rose, his muscles rippling as he strode around the circle. The early morning sun caught the grey fur on his back and turned it to liquid silver – a wolf god; the sight of him was enough – no member of the pack would stand against him. Tails wagged a little harder in acknowledgement of his mastery and magnificence.

Alexia watched this display; she had seen it many times. Her tongue flicked out and covered a yawn. She stretched and began to speak. All heads swivelled to this creature of lithe elegance, her white fur a dazzling blur as she too got to her feet.

'We are all here,' she said, 'save for Hero.'

'He must be brought to this Council.' Ajax's tone was grim – his teeth flashed their cutting edges. Alexia raised a paw to silence him; her ears twitched.

'He has arrived,' she said. A moment later from around the bend in the mountain came a slim dark wolf. His gaze fixed on Alexia's sharp intelligent face as he made his way to the circle, where he paused. Hero knew that the term 'policy meeting' was a euphemism. Such an event had one purpose only: to bring an errant wolf to book. His heart raced as he waited to be told what he must do. He would need all his wits if he were to avoid the ultimate punishment; banishment from the pack would mean an uncertain future with every hour of every day fraught with danger and loneliness. Starvation was an ugly word that lodged in his brain.

'You are late,' barked Ajax.

'I apologise,' began Hero, crawling into the submissive pose. 'I have had business matters to attend to.'

A titter went round the circle and the pack took the release of tension as an opportunity to lick their neighbour's face; they must keep their bonds strong. They knew what Hero was like.

'Business matters? Hmm.' Ajax's paw stroked his whiskered chin. All knew this was a sign that he was waiting for Alexia to speak.

'There are charges you must answer Hero. Come into the centre where you may be interrogated,' she said.

Hero wanted to turn and flee – those slanted eyes of hers with their strange white centres filled him with great dread. But he did not run. He walked to the chosen spot, his nails making soft clicks on the frozen ground. Ajax and Alexia sat side by side, their heads alert, their bushy tails curled around their bodies. Hero did likewise: it was important that he presented his case with confidence, not prone in front of the leaders. The other wolves too came into sitting position.

Alexia waited until the bustle had ceased, then said,

'These are the accusations laid against you. You must answer them all.

First, it is some time since you attended manoeuvre training, which as you know, all wolves must take part in regularly.

Second, you have made no contribution to the larder for weeks. You do not join the pack on hunting trips.

Third, you have been seen taking batches of young cubs to secret places.

These are all serious charges Hero. What have you to say?'

This last was accompanied with a growl and a snap of teeth. The fur on the back of Hero's neck stood up in black spikes at the menace directed towards him. He forced himself to return her stare:

'Let me explain...' he was cut short by a snarl from Ajax.

'We do not need to hear your excuses – you insolent young pup. We are here to decide what to do about you.'

'Please,' Hero stretched out a shaky paw, 'no excuses, just explanations.' He tilted his head to one side, an almost inaudible whine accentuating his plea.

Alexia's ears pricked forward and as Ajax in his fury was about to pounce on Hero, she put out a restraining paw.

'We will hear your "explanations",' she said, 'but be warned, what you say may not change anything for you.'

Hero gulped, but his tail wagged in recognition of her magnanimous gesture.

'I will take these matters in the order you have listed.' He licked his lips. 'It is true I have not been present at manoeuvre training but that does not mean that I have forgotten what I learnt as a young cub.'

'Doing, reinforces learning,' said Ajax with a touch of pomposity. Hero was surprised that Ajax remembered that.

'It makes the training and responses more...what's the word?' Ajax looked around hopefully.

'Automatic,' supplied Hero.

'Yes, hmm.' Ajax attended to a piece of fur that was not quite as pristine as it should be.

'Nevertheless,' Hero resumed, 'I hope to convince you that my time has not been wasted.' The looks he received were not encouraging but he rushed on.

'As regards the hunting trips, I may not have brought food to the pack,
but what I have done is to seek out storage places. I am sure the Controllers of the Larder will confirm that I have taken them to three or four areas where meat may be deposited and kept for weeks.'

He nodded in the direction of two senior wolves, one of whom, Deena,
drew back her lip as if about to snarl. The other, Samo, responded:
'Yes, that's true. Hero's been most helpful. He finds the best places, the
most secure.' Her whole body bobbed as if to reinforce her words.

Hero whined his thanks and thumped his tail in appreciation.

'Turning to the third issue – I take the little cubs to a quiet ground for educational purposes.'

'Educational?' blustered Ajax. 'What is your meaning?'

Hero took a breath. 'There are matters you should all know about.'

A dozen pairs of ears pricked forward. 'Some of my time is spent in communication with humans.'

A low growl of surprise and alarm went round the pack.

'In communication? How is that?' said Alexia, edging closer to Hero. 'We cannot speak their language.'

'It is not so difficult,' said Hero, 'a question of tuning in really. I have spent the last year or two making a study of what is called human psychology and behaviour patterns.'

'Psycho-babble,' shouted one of the wolves, breaking the rule that no wolf may speak unless invited to do so by the leaders. A rustle of unease went through the circle.

'Yes,' said Hero, 'some people call it that but an understanding of these 'masters of the universe' – as they see themselves, can only help our species.'

'How so?' asked Alexia.

'First, let me tell you what I know. This is important: wolves have a very bad image in the world of people. We are seen as aggressive, predatory, dangerous creatures to be feared.'

Ajax sat up straight. 'And what is wrong with that?'

'We need to be seen in a different light – to achieve something of the status of elephants, dolphins, even possibly the dog.'

Much ribaldry followed this, with calls of 'dogs are no more than craven wimps.'

'Like you Hero,' one shouted.

'Listen to me,' Hero got to his feet. 'In the world outside, everything changes constantly. The human population is increasing day by day. Our own species is diminishing steadily. We need to be seen as playing an essential role in the wild, and not so wild landscape. We must teach people to love us, to know our skills and see our usefulness to them, to want to protect us from extinction.'

There was a silence and Hero breathed deeply. 'Sniff the air my friends. We must all adapt or we will die.'

'How do we do that Hero?' Alexia's ears were well forward to catch every word.

'There are many ways. To start with, when I take the youngsters, I teach them to look for people in distress, walkers who have lost their way, those who have had accidents and need help.'

'What nonsense,' barked Ajax. 'How could we possibly assist these stupid ones?'

'It's a question of applying some intelligence; for instance, someone lost just needs to be shown the path; an injured person can be helped by taking a piece of clothing or belonging from them. One finds the rescue party and drops the article where it will be seen. There will be an individual amongst the rescuers who will eventually catch on and usually they say, 'I think the wolf is trying to tell us something.' Then one leads them to the injured party.'

Hero ceased speaking. He was exhausted. He could do no more – he had no idea what would happen to him. There was a stillness – it seemed as if his words had fallen into a void. Then Alexia stirred: her eyes glittered.

'When we gave you your name Hero, it was in jest.'

'Yes, I know, an ironic comment.'

'But no longer. You may well save our species.' She turned to the group of wolves.

'Pack,' she called, 'I give you Hero, the champion of all wolves. He is the wolf-man who has sniffed the air and will lead us in this new world. Show him your appreciation.'

As one, the wolves threw back their heads and howled into the morning sky. The sound echoed around the mountains and drifted down to the valley below.

INHERITANCE   by P.C.R. Penfold

I opened the door to the café, cosily lit on this dank afternoon. I had received a frantic call from my friend Martin less than half-an-hour ago, and I had driven as fast as I could to this place, not far from the manor house in which he and his mother lived. I searched the tables for him and couldn't believe it when a bespectacled man sitting in a shadowy corner caught my attention – a scruffy farmer's cap pulled down over his eyes, which peered out at me in a rather theatrical way.

'Why are you dressed like that?'

'Hallo Paul – I don't want to be recognised,' he hissed. I had to suppress a desire to laugh but did so to save his feelings.

'Those thick black glasses? Bit over the top, isn't it? And they make you more noticeable, not less. Although I will admit, I had to look twice, so what's the idea?'

'Get yourself some coffee, then please sit down and I'll tell you.'

I went to the counter and ordered a large coffee and a tasty looking wedge of carrot cake. I felt I was here for the long haul, especially as the drizzle outside had not eased.

'So, what's happened?'

'Wait until she's delivered your order.'

He took a sip from his cup with a hand that shook very slightly. I looked at him with raised eyebrows. He steadily returned my gaze, silently pleading for my patience. In a few minutes that seemed longer, the waitress came with my order and the bill. Martin's eyes still held mine as he began.

'I had to get out. There was no-one I could talk to back at the house. The staff are probably going crazy by now, what with Grandad and everything.'

'You'd better start from the beginning old chap. You're not making a lot of sense.'

'Right. Here it is. My grandfather called me to come into the library. Pretty serious stuff I thought, probably about the Will. We both sat down, and he picked up a narrow box. "I have something to give to you," he said, and he opened it. He held it out to me like it was a precious jewel on a velvet pillow. I suppose you might say: "reverently."'

'And what was it?'

'I'll show you in a moment. I don't want anyone to see. I have it here.' He patted the pocket of his coat.

'Show me,' I said, 'pass it under the table.'

It was a jewelled dagger. I studied it discreetly, keeping it by my side under the table. The blade was not very long, and the handle was set with diamonds in a sweeping curlicue, reminding me of Poirot's moustache. Then the top part, which was above the cross piece, was in the form of an old man's head with a flowing beard. And it looked as if it was solid gold. There were some other stones, deep yellow in colour which I thought might also be diamonds. The whole thing was about 7 or 8 inches long. It was beautiful and unlike anything I had ever seen. I passed it back.

'It looks very valuable. Not very practical as a dagger though. Ornamental, I suppose. What's the story? Why did he give it to you?'

'My grandfather said my father should have been the one to present it to me now that I'm thirty. It must have been significant in some way, like an heirloom, although I'm certain my mother has never mentioned it. My father was killed in the war, so Grandfather said he knew that on this day, my birthday, he would be the one to give it to me. It all sounded terribly formal – significant you might say. But that's not it.'

'Right,' I said, not thinking anything was 'right' at the moment. 'Go on.'

'While my grandfather was holding it out to me, he had this enigmatic smile. I took it from him. Then, I had what I can only describe as a vision, right in front of me in the space between the two of us. Through a haze, like a mist, I saw a baby boy, growing through childhood, through marriage to my mother, then on through a war which blew him to bits. It lasted for less than a minute, I think. From photographs, I recognised the man as my father. I swear, I have never experienced anything like it in my life, it was so weird. When it cleared and I looked across at my grandfather, he was still sitting, gazing at me with this fixed expression. Only now, I realised to my horror, that it was a rictus grin. I didn't know what to think, there was blood pouring from the side of his neck. I thought it must have been me, that I had killed him while this thing, this vision, was happening, but when I looked at the dagger in my hand, it was clean. I ran to him, but there was nothing I could do. He was definitely dead. I was horrified! I panicked. I put the dagger back in the box and ran; picked up this stuff I'm wearing from the junk room and ran. Now, I don't know what the hell to do.'

Nor did I. I just knew that running away was not the answer.

'You have to tell the police. You have to face it out. If the dagger wasn't covered in blood, then you didn't kill him. It could have been a bullet, maybe a dart − anything. Someone else. All I know is that on TV, the ones that run away cause more problems for themselves. It's a sign of guilt; you have to go back.'

'But they'll arrest me...'

'...and then they'll let you go.'

'What about the vision?'

'You probably dropped off for a second, epilepsy maybe. I don't know.'

'Will you look after the dagger for me?'

'I guess so. It doesn't seem like any ordinary dagger though, does it.'

'Will you come back with me?'

'I suppose so.'

We left money on the table and went out into the grey drizzle and into my car. I put the boxed dagger in the glove compartment. The silence was palpable between us and I was glad the drive was only five minutes, which he had apparently walked, or more likely, he had run. I turned into his drive and the beautiful old stone house came into view. It all looked so peaceful with its neat gardens and glittering windows, wearing that unhurried permanence that old, stately homes seem to emanate.

Two other cars were parked at the front. I persuaded him to remove his ridiculous disguise, then we clambered out of the low seats and Martin led the way. We were greeted by his mother who seemed to have been waiting for us.

'I'm so glad you're back, Martin. Where have you been?'

'Just fancied a stroll, Mother and bumped into Paul here. Is something wrong?'

'You'd better come and see for yourself. It's your grandfather. I'm so sorry, you had better prepare yourself for a shock.'

We followed her into the library; the oppressive atmosphere of death had already seeped through my skin as I tried to look innocent and whatever 'normal' should look like. In the face of what I had just heard, an ordinary expression seemed to have escaped me. Was this what guilt looked like? I stole a glance at Martin, hoping to learn what his face reflected. His expression was that of ferocious concentration and I felt the intensity of his fear.

'Oh my God!'

Martin's explosion of emotion sounded utterly genuine as I was sure it was. I too, gasped, hand to mouth. The old man was now lying prostrate on the couch, a doctor at his head looking on with a grave expression.

'I'm afraid he's dead. It must have been shortly after you left him. I'm so sorry Martin, I know he was like a father to you after your father died.'

Martin and his mother hugged in silent, mutual comfort. I turned to the doctor.

'What did he die of?'

'A blood clot in the neck, I'm afraid. A bit like a stroke; he would have had very few symptoms.'

'Would the clot have burst through the skin? You know – blood?'

'No, no, there was no blood. That's the problem really. The blood clotted and was unable to continue to circulate.'

I looked at Martin. 'I'm sorry for your loss, Martin. And you too Dame Ashworth.' I went to him and hugged him.

'Some vision,' I whispered, 'I think you should get rid of that dagger as quickly as possible. It's cursed!'

Martin looked dazed but had the presence of mind to nod. 'Cursed, definitely cursed.'

THE FISHING TRIP   by S.F. Formi

There was a stillness, almost complete, as if life was extinct. But he knew this moment and waited: a sudden plop in the water and the river rippled into larger and larger circles. Years ago, he had learnt the skill of concealing himself, becoming invisible by remaining motionless, holding his breath, so now he waited. Would there be a bite? But no, the rod did not twitch; there was no panicked jumping in the depths below.

He let the breath go in a sigh, scanning the countryside around him as he did so. In the distance, the early sun was turning the hills to gold, and streaks of blue and pink dispersed a grey sky. But closer, downriver, a thin mist played like crêpe ribbons. No movement; no sound. Jack's eyes narrowed, his senses alert as he searched the landscape. Another sigh, nothing, nobody: just him and the world. A soft breeze stroked his cheek, curled the greying hair as the reeds behind him whispered their secrets.

Securing the rod on its rest, he leant back on the grassy bank. He'd chosen this spot for the protection it gave him from the elements; it suited him, this place, he thought, as he unpacked his rucksack; old and fraying at the edges, it was still sturdy enough to hold what he needed.

First came the plastic box containing his food, next there was a flask, and then the small blanket to spread everything on. In the bottom somewhere, lay the paper plates and few bits of cutlery he always carried with him, plus a battered hat. His chair was of the sort that folded up so it could be carried on his back. It stood ready, close to the water with the paraphernalia of rod and creel.

He released the lid on the sandwich box and reached for the contents: cold bacon and tomato, larded with ketchup between two hunks of bread – breakfast. For the moment nothing else mattered, he savoured the flavours in his mouth: the saltiness of the bacon, the stickiness of the sauce dribbling down his chin − savoured too, the sensation of complete oneness with his surroundings. His ears picked up the twitter of the reed buntings in the rushes and the croak of a nearby bullfrog. Tea from the thermos, hot and strong, builders' tea, washed down the first meal of the day. His hand reached again for the backpack and brought out a pair of binoculars.

Scanning the horizon, he was reassured; the mist had lifted and he had a clear view across the river and up to the low hills beyond. Coming to his feet, he swung round and checked the area behind him: all clear. Brushing the crumbs from his Guernsey jumper, he stretched and flecked his arms before returning to the rod bobbing gently in the water. The portable chair creaked as his body settled back into the seat. Peace, perfect peace.

His mind wandered back to the old days in the East End. Not much peace in those days, his mouth twisted into a grin as the memories piled in: that adrenalin rush when you were on a job; the camaraderie, all working against the clock, knowing so much depended on their synchronised skills. Tap, tap, hush, and listen to the cogs falling into place. And then that moment, the thrill, the excitement when the door swung open and all was revealed. Of course, there were those times when it didn't all go smoothly. He frowned and straightened, and again his eyes darted here, there and everywhere. Just at that moment the fishing line tensed and a splashing began.

It was a wily character and took some time to land, but then there it was, a fat, sleekly glistening, brown trout. He gazed at it with satisfaction a moment before placing it in his creel. Content, he pushed back in his seat, retrieving the creased canvas hat from his bag, which he jammed on his head. The sun's rays wrapped a blanket of warmth round his prone body. Jack's limbs relaxed, his legs spreading wide, his features softened. He slept.

He awoke with a start; the line was jerking again. Another plump, shiny fish joined its twin. He glanced at his watch; much later than he'd thought. In that case it was time to eat. Opening a second bag, he pulled out a portable barbecue resembling a toolbox. He lit the charcoal with an old cigarette lighter, and when all was ready, he flicked open his pocketknife. The blade slid smoothly through the belly of each fish exposing the bloody innards. Once gutted and washed clean in river water, he stuffed the gaping holes with some wild garlic he'd found on the way. When the coals were glowing, he added the fish and watched a moment as the skin began to crisp and sizzle. Quite soon a smoky aroma began to tease his senses. Now and again the pungent smell of the wild garlic broke through; he licked his lips. Anticipation was almost the best part.

Solitude, not loneliness, he said to himself. And solitude is all I want these days. He flipped the fish over with his knife and tested the flesh with a light prick. There was a sound behind him.

'That looks good,' said a voice.

Jack turned slowly. His face remained calm but his heart thumped against his ribs. A man stood there; he was as long and lithe as Jack, his face as craggy, but unlike Jack he sported a three-piece suit.

Jack looked him up and down. 'Not come to fish then Fred?' he said.

The other grinned. Jack turned back to the barbecue. 'Looks like this will all be wasted,' he said.

'No,' said Fred, hitching his trousers as he bent to squat down beside Jack's chair, 'no rush. Enjoy your meal.'

Jack nodded and produced two plates from the backpack, placing a trout on each. 'Here,' he said, handing one over. Rummaging again in the bag he brought out some knives and forks, 'always carry spare irons.'

Fred sprawled on the grass and speared a piece of fish. He closed his eyes. 'This is good Jack, very good.'

Jack nodded again. 'It shouldn't have happened you know,' he said, his glance sliding across to his companion.

'You sent her some money, didn't you?' said Fred, 'quite a lot in fact.'

'Least I could do. She had to look after him, didn't she?' He heaved a big sigh. 'We always said no violence, no harm. Didn't work out that time though.'

'No,' said Fred, picking up another morsel of the trout. 'It's all over for him now anyway. You heard?'

'Yeah, I heard.'

'But what you did – calling the ambulance, the money she got from you – all that will put you in a better standing.'

'It's no matter Fred. I'm tired: tired of watching and hiding. I've had my good moments.' He picked up his fork. 'Let's eat up and then I'm ready to go. I'll give you no trouble.'

There was silence as the two men cleaned the bones of every bit of the pinkish moist flesh. The sun slid lower in the sky, shadows began to form around the two shapes hunched over their plates, the river darkened and the birds hushed their chatter as if waiting for a change to come.

TRUNK CALL   by P.C.R. Penfold

The trunk was oblong, solid, and heavy and it sat in the middle of Chris's dining room. He felt its presence had assumed a sinister air. He had tried to refuse acceptance of it at the front door, but the massively built, dark skinned gentleman had given the impression that he did not understand and would not be argued with, as he pushed his way past him. Chris did his best to bar his way.

'It's not for me! That's not my name on the label.'

'No.' The man had replied as he kicked open the dining room door and plonked the trunk down as if it were merely a bag of shopping. Then he quickly turned to leave. Chris was so surprised, he couldn't think of what to say and so he repeated lamely to the man's retreating back: 'Hey, that's not my name. It's not for me.'

The man just repeated over his shoulder, one hand raised as if he were agreeing, but was in fact disagreeing. 'No,' he repeated and left.

Chris sat and looked at the trunk, noting its evident age and that it was made of thick brown leather with reinforced metal corners and extra struts. It was secured with three leather straps which ran all the way around it, ending with three large rusty buckles. He studied the thin cardboard label which was attached with string to the buckle in the middle. It didn't look as tattered as he would have expected and was written in ink.

He read it again. 'Adam Peabody,' followed by the address of the Victorian house in which he was living and renting. 'Never heard of him,' he muttered.

It looked difficult to unfasten; the buckles didn't appear to have been undone in quite a while. He fetched a beer from the kitchen, flicking off the cap with his key ring opener and taking a thoughtful swig. It didn't help; no inspiration followed and the box still looked ominous, so he kicked it. It was very hard, as his softly clad foot confirmed. He set the beer down and took a closer look. There was no slack in the strap to release the buckle prong and no suppleness left in the crusty looking leather. He could just get a fingernail under the strap. He checked the label again, turning it over to make sure there was no 'return to sender' message. Nothing.

Back to the kitchen, this time to get a carving knife. Curiosity had now won over integrity, as well as the slight nervousness that had first gripped him. The long thin blade slipped under the strap and by tilting it slightly upwards, he could saw it with short awkward strokes. It was several minutes before the released strap clanked to the floor. One down, two to go. He continued diligently until all three straps lay spread out on either side of the trunk. The lid was one which neatly overhung the body of the box without the need for a hinge. He pulled at it with both hands and levered it off successfully. He peered inside, half expecting something nasty to leap out and grab him.

At that moment, there was a sharp rapping sound. Chris jumped back in fright until he realised that the sound had not come from the trunk, but from the front door. With a last puzzled look at the contents, Chris went to open it. A tall man stood there, dressed in a weirdly old-fashioned suit with a stiff collar and a top hat, a cane in his hand raised and ready to knock again.

'My name is Adam Peabody,' the man said, and Chris smiled, visualising the broken straps lying across the floor. 'I believe you have been delivered of a trunk belonging to me?' Before Chris could confirm, Mr Peabody continued, 'I sent it to this address which was my home in 1855. May I come in?'

Chris nodded and stepped aside, admiring the man's amazing costume. He looked like an actor who was still wearing Victorian fancy dress.

'It contains valuable research documents of my time machine model and plans, he continued, glancing around with interest. 'I have spent some time travelling in order to retrieve it. May I please have it back now?'

Chris stared in shock. 'Really? Are you kidding me?'

'I don't understand your language, young man, but if you mean am I telling the truth, how do you think I got here?'

'Beats me! What are you going to do now?'

'Build another machine of course. Would you be so kind as to strap it up again? You seem to have wantonly destroyed the straps I thought were so secure.'

Chris scurried off to find some leather belts, at least enough to secure the trunk for transportation. Then a thought struck him. He returned to the dining room with two belts.

'If you have just arrived, where is the machine?'

'In the cellar, where I built it.'

'I haven't got a cellar.'

'Yes, you have. There's a trap door in the hall, hidden under that carpet,' he waved his cane in a vaguely circular motion.

'But you came in the front door. And the trunk was delivered.'

Mr Peabody sighed, as if talking to a very stupid child. 'I sent the trunk on ahead, bit of an experiment, and it got lost in the post as you might say. But I arrived, with my machine, on target. In other words, I didn't go anywhere, just jumped forward a few years. What year is this, by the by?

'2020. But you didn't just rise up through a hole in the floor. I'd have seen you!'

'No, of course not! How long have you lived here?'

'Well, actually, just a few weeks. So how did you get out of the cellar?'

'Another trap door, my innocent friend. It comes up in the garden, which I have to say, needs a good deal of work. Fortunately, no brambles to clamber through, but my word, so much long grass and nasty weeds.'

Peabody took the opportunity to brush his cuffs and study his clothing
more carefully. 'Now, are you going to help me or not?'

Chris looked at Mr Peabody and shook his head, not in dissent, more in amazement.

'It looks as if I have a house guest. Would you like a cup of tea?'

'Yes, please, what an amazing luxury! I think I shall like staying with you, sir.'

LEGACY

by S.F. Formi

Rain sluices down the windowpane, obscuring the view of the countryside as it flashes past. The grey skies and endless down-pouring are becoming oppressive. To add to my mood, the train then slows with a screech that sets my teeth on edge. I look round at my fellow passengers, not too many of them as I have chosen to travel first class for this momentous journey: momentous for me that is.

Opposite me sits a middle-aged couple; their stiff bodies and tight expressions remind me of Annabel and Jonathan. I flick my gaze away to divert my thoughts. There are two other people, businessmen by the way their eyes are glued to their laptops, fingers flying across the keyboards. They are in a world apart: the passing landscape, visible or not, as now, would fail to take their attention from their computers. I am drawn back to the two facing me. The woman is speaking, 'I'm worried about how Norma will take it,' she says, a look of appeal on her face. The man, her husband I assume, sniffs and turns away.

'Nothing to be done,' he says. The woman's face relapses into its former expression: the mouth a straight line matching the one across her forehead.

The stations slide past, one after the other: one hour to go. My stomach is a tight ball inside me. The sick feeling is with me again. I've had it since receiving the letter. I look at the woman opposite again and remember my last visit to Annabel. She was not far from the end and I'd thought she was sleeping. The memory is so strong it feels as if I am back in that room. I close my eyes but cannot stop the events of that moment crowding in on me.

The room is full of a soft quiet; there is a gentle purr from some machine or other in the corner. Annabel's breathing is almost undetectable; the pure white sheet hardly stirs. I pick up my phone to check what is going on at work. There is a slight movement and a whisper. Her voice barely reaches me and in surprise I look up.

'Darling,' she begins. The use of the endearment sounds odd: I have never heard it from her before, 'we were wrong to do what we did,' she pauses for breath, while I struggle to understand what she is saying. Is her mind wandering? 'The wrong reasons I'm afraid.' She reaches for my hand and, mystified I look into those blue eyes, still bright, still beautiful, though sunk deep into the head. 'I should have spoken.' The voice is weak, the strangled vowels somewhat muted with age and illness. 'You had a right...' the words tail off as her breath fails her and she drifts into sleep again.

I wait around for a while but she does not wake before they ask me to leave, lest I tire her. I pad through the silent corridors, my feet sinking into the deep carpets, my eyes straying to the works of art decorating the pristine white walls. It is as if the occupants are being gently cosseted through their last dark days; plush cushions and curtains that whisper on brass rails ensure that they leave the world as they lived in it. Luxury surrounds me, but I am used to that.

The end comes a few days later and I can feel nothing but frustration that I have no knowledge of what she wanted to tell me. What was it she should have said?

Some six weeks later, I am drinking my coffee at the breakfast table and puzzling over a speech I am intending to make. A heavy package drops through the letterbox. It is the Will. Though my friends had always teased me about my so-called 'heiress' status, it had never seemed a reality to me. Some deep instinct, perhaps a legacy of a loveless childhood, told me that those sweeping grounds with their manor of mellowed brick would never belong to me. And so it is. The Will is clear on that; there is 'provision' for me but the estate passes elsewhere. But it is the contents of the letter accompanying it that shakes me to the point where, later, I shut myself away from contact with friends and colleagues; work is abandoned.

As I read, much that was puzzling or lacking in my life is explained. The first bombshell hits me; I sink into my chair, my thoughts spinning chaotically. The letter states that I, along with my twin brother, was adopted at birth. But what crushes me more than that is the information, baldly stated in Annabel's spidery writing, that the adoption came about because of Jonathan's desire for an heir, a male heir of course. The authorities would not allow twins to be split, she writes, so I had to come too. My mouth twists into a bitter grimace: I was the unwanted add-on. So much now seems clear to me. Even as a young child I was aware that Ben was treated differently, but then at the age of five he died of a rare disease. A few years later I was sent away to school, spending the holidays either at school or with the families of friends.

I take a deep breath to steady myself. Of course, as I grew up, I realised not all families are close but somehow, I had always known that there was something very wrong between my parents and myself. The nagging feeling that I did not belong drove me to my current career; to make a difference, to become someone. I became a political activist.

As I digest the news over the coming weeks, I realise I must now discover more about myself; where I came from; who my real parents were. And then the other question, the big one: Why?

So here I am. This journey is a quest to answer some of those questions. What will I learn? I straighten up and try to control the fluttering in my stomach. I must be ready for whatever comes. And now my station is coming into view. Very soon I will, for the first time, see my birth mother. Excitement and fear mingle together as I gather my belongings and the train grinds to a halt.

A DAY AT THE CINEMA   by P.C.R. Penfold

I'm not sure whose idea it was to go to the cinema but I admit I regret it now. I can't remember what the film was called, but it was glamorous, you know, lots of posh cars racing about chasing each other and women draping themselves all over the men. Anyway, I told Darius that I needed a pee, which was true. I stuck my elbow in his side and whispered, 'I have to go to the Ladies,' but he just ignored me. I asked him to move his legs out of the way so that I could get past him and he still ignored me; that idiot would not move, his eyes were glued to Brigitte Bardot or whoever she was, and it made me mad: madder than I'd ever been.

I trod on his foot as I struggled out to find the toilets and you know what? He barely grunted! I found the loos and rinsed my hands and that's when I saw it, just lying on the side where someone had left it. It was a rather fancy looking letter opener. Well, I couldn't resist it, could I! It was nicely ornamental on the handle, shiny silver with a raised pattern and then a long strong point. So, I picked it up and popped it in my handbag; there was absolutely no-one about, which was lucky.

I made my way back past the grumpy people who had to move their knees out of the way for me again and I sat down next to Darius. I say to him, 'Miss me?' and he just grunts. Yes, again! His eyes still glued to the screen. So I tried once more; I wanted to give him a second chance. 'I said... did you miss me?'

He looked at me as if he couldn't remember my name. 'Shut up! I'm trying to watch the film!' is what he said. And that's when I flipped. I took the letter opener out of my bag and I looked at it, then I stuck it into his side as hard as I could, and then for good measure, I twisted it. I pulled it out and wiped the blood on his sleeve as he sagged back in his seat.

I noticed his eyes had sort of glazed over. I thought to myself, 'I'd better get out of here, a bit sharpish!' He didn't look too good, you see. Then I had another brilliant idea. It's not my letter opener, perhaps I'll just go and put it back. I had to annoy all those people again, getting past their knees. But then, 'it's all right, I've got my back to them and it's dark, so they can't identify me.' See, I was quite clever, wasn't I? So anyway, I popped the letter opener back by the basin in the loos, gave it a bit of a rinse first, then left before everyone came out after the film finished, and got the bus home.

It seemed like ages before the cops came and picked me up; I suppose after a bit, his mum probably reported him missing. He would have been the only one left in the pictures wouldn't he. Ha! So here I am with just a few memories of all those years ago and nothing better to do than stare at that radiator like it's the bloody television. They say I'll never be allowed out of this place, because I don't know if I'm mad or if I was just dreaming. Perhaps I made it all up; I don't really know anymore.

A SWEET MOMENT   by S.F. Formi

The restaurant had the buzzy, bustling sound that a good eating establishment has. The ambience was warm and relaxed with candlelight flickering and glowing on the polished cutlery. She was glad that there was no piped music, no jangling strings or endless crooning, to play on nerves already strung taut.

She had chosen to sit at the far end of the room, where she could see the door. The table was laid for two, silver cutlery wrapped in creamy crisp linen napkins. A folded newspaper lay between the place settings.

She saw him as he was handing over his coat; she caught the flash of his smile when he turned to the waitress and watched the colour mount in the young girl's face. She knew that smile, that attentive look so full of charm.

She picked up her glass and sipped her dry martini. The sharp liquid was bracing, fortifying.

He made his way through the tables, nodding and smiling at the other diners. He reached her with arms outstretched and she was folded into his warm, expensive embrace.

'You look wonderful,' he said. 'How long's it been?' He settled into his seat, picked up the menu and began looking at it.

'Ten years,' she said.

'Ten? That many?'

'How's things?' she said

'Good, really good,' he glanced up from the menu, 'I'm on the Board now. Chairman's knocking on, so maybe in a couple of years...' He nodded, his face full of anticipation.

'And you?' he said, 'how's the bank?'

'Oh, I left there soon after...you know.'

'I think I'll start with the mussels,' he murmured gazing at the menu, 'so where are you now? What are you into these days?' not looking up.

'Well, I suppose you could say that I'm into murder these days.'

His head jerked up, 'What?'

'I joined the Met. I've done all right actually.'

'Really? I wouldn't have thought...'

'No.' She angled the newspaper so that he could read the headline where she'd folded it. She watched as he leant forward, the black, silky mop of hair falling, almost, into his eyes – as it always did. Her stomach clenched.

'I don't understand.' He looked confused, strained.

'I'm part of that: "Met sets up new cold case team",' she gave a little shrug, her eyes remaining on his face. 'By the way, did you ever re-marry? Your secretary? We couldn't possibly, at the time – it might implicate you in some way, and I was so young. That's what you said, wasn't it?'

She paused, fingering her glass and watched the colour drain from his face.

'And of course, you were grieving.'

The handsome features, the firm jaw line, seemed somehow to have become haggard and slack. She saw beads of perspiration begin to appear on his forehead.

He pushed his chair back. It made an ugly scraping noise. 'I have to go. I'm...not feeling well.'

She watched as he stumbled through the tables, this time not looking at the occupants of the chairs he bumped into.

She leaned back, a sigh escaping. Picking up the martini, she let the golden liquid swirl round her mouth. Her stomach muscles loosened. There was no hurry: she had everything she needed, now.

NEVER GO BACK   by S.F. Formi

The car slowed to a halt beside the bus stop. For some minutes the driver sat motionless in his seat, his thoughts far away. Coming back to the present he took in his surroundings; nothing much had changed here – fields of scrub and mud and little else, a couple of sagging farm buildings and a few wind-torn trees.

'God-forsaken dump,' he muttered. His eyes drifted back to the deserted bus stop. His face tightened as he remembered the cold needles of rain that had pierced his skin that day as they waited for the bus to come: the man beside him pacing nervously up and down.

With a shake of his head, James let in the clutch and drove off. A few miles further on he turned off the road onto a short drive, pulling up in front of a large grey building. He sat there unmoving as the past again poured over him.

'C'mon Jimmy.' He heard again the rough accents and felt the pull on his arm as he stumbled up the steps.

This time James walked briskly into the building. Once inside, the memories engulfed him. He stood still as the smell of over-cooked cabbage and the damp chill of an under-heated room came back to him. Panic threatened him as he remembered the woman coming from behind the desk to take his hand.

'You'll be all right here Jimmy. They'll look after you now,' the man had said.

The shriek of despair echoed again in his head. He had tried to run after his father. He'd heard the scrape, scrape of his boots on the uncarpeted floor. Leaving him.

A woman was looking at him, her eyebrows raised in query. James brought himself back to the present and told her what he was there for. A few minutes later he found himself standing inside a small square room containing a minimum of furniture, some of it very dilapidated.

An old man sat over by the window. He turned as James came further into the room.

'Who are you?' the voice tugged at James's memory, though it trembled slightly.

'You don't know me?' he said.

'How would I know you? I've never blooming well seen you before. People in and out of this place all the time. I don't know...'

James stepped a bit closer. Cleaning his glasses with a handkerchief, the old man hooked them over his ears and peered at James.

'It's not...it's not...Jimmy? Is it you, Jimmy?' His voice was breaking up and a shaky hand reached out towards James. It lay in the space between them, untouched. There was a short silence, then, 'I can't believe it. After all...'

'After all these years, yes,' said James, 'and the name is James now.'

'How did you know where I was?'

'I've known your whereabouts for years. Not difficult. You're hardly a great traveller. You were living in that sheltered housing complex until a few months ago.'

'That's right. So why didn't you come then? This place is the end of the
road for me.' There was a bitter tone to the laugh.

'I know what you mean. I remember how it felt too,' said James, his gaze steady on the old man. There was silence.

'I had no choice son. After your mother died, things were so hard, very hard.' He gave James a sharp look. 'You don't look as if you've done so bad. Smart suit, posh name. What do you do with yourself?'

73

He doesn't get it, thought James. *He's no idea what I went through.*

To the old man he said, 'I'm a barrister. If you ever read a decent newspaper, you might have seen my name once or twice.'

Eyes widening, the old man repeated, 'a barrister? In London? There's money in that.' Then, 'why did you come, now?'

James looked at him. Suddenly his shoulders sagged. *Why had he come? What was the point?*

Abruptly he turned, pulled the door open and walked from the room. His father's tremulous words followed him, 'I had no choice. Every day Jimmy, every day, I thought of you.'

As he walked through the reception, James became aware for the first time of the changes. In place of the dark gloomy pictures and stiff benches, there were now comfortable armchairs and a big bowl of fresh flowers to welcome the visitor.
James hurried to the car, fiddled with some buttons on the CD player,
then roared out of the drive, the thumping beat of the Rolling Stones,

"Satisfaction", driving the whirlwind of emotions out of his head.

MISSION TO HELL   by P.C.R. Penfold

Carlton checked his instruments and despite an ineffectual tap on the dial with his knuckle, he could plainly see that they were losing altitude. He turned to his co-pilot, Simon.

'Can you see where we are on the map?'

'Not exactly. And my head is thumping.'

'Mine too. I think I blacked out for a second.'

'Well, we're out of contact now.'

'To hell with this secret mission!'

'Get the binoculars, he should be down there somewhere.'

The terrain they were instructed to search and land in was not an easy one on which to bring down the helicopter. On visual only, Carlton circled to identify the exact location of their target. He strained to recognise the hill contours to match the map in front of him, as he skimmed low over the treetops.

'No sign of agriculture or buildings, but that depression over there is on the map. We're back on track, I think.'

Simon wiped away the dampness that had gathered on his forehead with the back of his hand. His headache persisted and he guessed it must be the atmosphere, which was heavy and cloying. He reached for a bottle of water and took a careful swig, his eyes all the time sweeping and searching for their prey. He handed the bottle to Carlton.

'The instruments are all over the place; they're working now but there's something wrong.'

'Let's land. Look, over there, there's a plateau. That'll do and we could continue searching on foot. What do you think?'

'Too risky. I'll take her off to the west in a figure of eight and we'll have another look. I really don't like the idea of being on the ground with him. Load the gun with a double dose of sedative and we'll try to hit him from up here.'

Carlton felt the weight of the responsibility as oppressively as the heat. He knew that their failure would be concealed beneath a stack of paperwork lies, and their success also would be a well-kept secret, as unremarked as failure. Even so, questions would be asked about their actions and he had to be able to give intelligent and reasoned responses.

He circled again, noting the lack of cover for their target, and the ground which was stony and uneven and not at all suitable for landing. Over his shoulder, he checked their equipment: stun gun; hand and foot manacles; the cage. This was a precaution to protect against assault from the prisoner after they had him in the helicopter. They also had a trolley which could be mechanically raised to assist with loading the body directly into the cage and from there, into the back of the helicopter.

'I see movement! I don't think it's wind from the rotors, it's hard to tell. I saw a flash of yellow as well. Don't spook him! We could still go back to the plateau and find him on foot, couldn't we?'

'No, I've already told you. That's about 500 yards away and we could lose him in that time. Look, there he goes, he's sort of running now, but quite slowly. I'll turn so you can get a better aim. Shoot! Shoot now!'

Simon fired and hit the target between the shoulder blades. Two more stumbling steps and their quarry dropped to the ground.

'Good work. Now we can land on the plateau. My God, the instruments are going crazy! What's going on with this machine?'

'Do your best Carlton. My head is splitting. This atmosphere definitely doesn't suit me.'

'Nor me, but not much more to do now.' He made a bumpy landing, jolting them both. 'Help me with the trolley and don't forget the manacles.'

They hurried over to their prey, the trolley bouncing and jostling over the uneven ground.

'I wish we could be more sure he'll still be asleep. No way of knowing how much sedative we should have given.'

Finally, they could inspect him. He was lying quite still and breathing steadily, but rapidly. Nothing on Earth quite resembled him: he had the physique of a man but he wasn't. His skin was pale yellow and tough looking. His face was broad, with a non-protruding nose and a small pouting mouth. Also, he was completely hairless. His legs were well-muscled but had not functioned well when he was running; they were the same length as his arms. His body was much smaller than either Carlton or Simon, he was no more than 5 feet tall and weighing probably less than 8 stone.

They had no trouble lifting him onto the trolley, but seeing the creature's round green eyes flicker open, Simon quickly manacled his hands and feet, exchanging a satisfied grin with Carlton. They pushed the trolley and its unearthly cargo back to the helicopter, easier now with some weight on it, and stowed it straight into the cage and then into the back of the helicopter. Simon proffered some gum and they both relaxed briefly in the afterglow of achievement. Then Carlton felt himself sway.

'Are you all right?'

'It's my head. How's yours?'

'Pounding. Shall we sit for a bit before going back?'

Carlton nodded and they climbed into their seats, exhausted and sweating.

'D'you think they will ever tell us what this is?' Simon waved a hand at the inert yellow figure. 'You know, like, where it came from?'

'I doubt it. But I don't think he's from round here.' He laughed despite his head throbbing and now feeling queasy as well. 'Let's get him back to base.'

He felt more like sleeping than flying, but he said nothing, not wanting to worry Simon.

77

Again, he had a brief sensation of having been unconscious, just for a few seconds. With a tremendous effort of concentration, he got the helicopter airborne. Ignoring the lurching feeling in his stomach, he checked the instruments, only to confirm his worst fears; despite the initial successful lift off, they were again losing altitude. Then he heard the blades falter, then falter again, the noise hitting his eardrums in a staccato drumbeat to match the thumping in his head. He turned to speak to Simon, panic ready to swamp him, but to his dismay he saw that Simon was unconscious, his head tilted back, his eyes and mouth wide open.

Worse even than that, was an unbelievably horrific sight: behind Simon's inert form stood the yellow creature, un-manacled and uncaged, his features bland and unreadable. Carlton froze as panic and fear crept through his whole being. The helicopter was completely out of control as was the evil figure behind him. He could do nothing to save either his mission or himself, as the helicopter swooped into a death dive. He felt an unbearable heat overtaking him and his cargo. The aircraft shuddered, like a living creature, as it plunged to the earth and erupted in flames, taking all three to an anonymous grave.

A TIMELESS TRYST   by P.C.R. Penfold

From my elevated position of seventeen hands above the ground, I fill my lungs with the scent of pine needles. Oscar, my bay horse snorts in that comical way: blowing out through both his nose and his lips, making them vibrate and shudder. Sitting here alone, with only the sound of his syncopated hooves, I attempt to imitate it with my voice. Oscar's ears twitch back and forth and I imagine he is laughing at me. I gently press my heels to his sides and he responds, his swaying head lifting and his steps abandoning their rhythm in exchange for a canter.

Trees are to my left and right – all towering and straight, majestic pines, but our path through them is wide, the floor soft and springy, dense with years of cast-off spines, now as brown as bog-water. I can see the gate ahead, meant to keep in the deer but I have often seen them leap right over it. I sense their presence, deeper in the wood by shrubs and ponds, guarding their privacy in silent groups. I squeeze my heels again and crouch low, shortening the reins, my knees pressing closer now as we clear the gate. That instant of flying is exhilarating to us both, and after, our pace steadies to a trot on the scrubland we now cross.

This also has a wide and worn pathway where others before me, before this special day, have walked or ridden. Perhaps armies have marched this route with hopes or fears in their hearts. Perhaps highwaymen have lingered, springing out on the mailmen or wielding a gun at passing strangers to rob them of their jewellery. I can see no-one, just the meadows unrolling before me and the hills beyond, like great green and grey waves climbing to the horizon, concealing lanes and hedgerows, woodlands and farms. Who knows the secret lives of others? Babies born, loved ones dying and maybe less innocent dramas unfolding. The world keeps on turning, filled with plots and schemes as well as simple pursuits for survival.

My daydreaming has caused Oscar to slow to a walk, and he snatches at mouthfuls of grass. Time is passing and I remind myself that, if I should arrive after dark then the impact of surprise will be less. I want to be seen, horse and rider breeching the hill and growing in size as I near his house. I tell Oscar that our destination is not so far, a mere two hours now, and I gently kick his belly to advance our speed. His nodding head lifts, as if he too can see beyond the hills. My journey has an ancient goal. I go to meet my lover. My heart quickens as the house comes into view. This will be where our new life begins.

POD LIFE   by P.C.R. Penfold

I stepped out of my sanitised pod and stretched, revelling in the feeling for just a few moments, of my limbs returning to life before memory flooded in to grab at my gut. My release from the pod had come early by 48 hours for a reason. I could only imagine bad things.

After the virus had wiped out three-quarters of the world's population, the universe had learned to pull together: just in time before more disasters struck. It hadn't been fast; it wasn't as if we had all been wiped out overnight. No. It had been insidious: a creeping destruction, almost unnoticed, before death had reached epidemic proportions. No vaccine was effective because the fatalities had many faces: the causes explained away quite rationally at first: heart attacks and similar conditions, although some people theorised a foreign incursion: a virus from space falling with the rain.

Allergies: that was another theory. Our immune systems were damaged, and intolerances were rife. At least that was more feasible than poisoned rain...or was it? Others pointed accusingly at the minute particles of plastic in everything we were eating and breathing. When it wasn't harming us directly through the deliberate introduction into skin products, teabags and toothpaste, then it was killing us indirectly: when it entered the food chain in plants, fish and meat. Maybe it had damaged our immune systems.

Despite social media, it seemed a long time before the death toll was flagged up as sinister, since it also took different people in different ways. Obviously, the old, infirm and the very young were the first to die, but when was that not the case? There seemed to be no cohesion of diagnosis.

We were destroying the environment, and little had been done to alleviate or reduce the impact of mankind. Nor had anyone made enough links to our interdependence on the world of insects and biodynamics to stop our selfish destruction of the planet. So, the cause was concealed behind a multitude of possibilities, all of which had their part to play. The virus was just the last straw.

Adding to the problem had been our ostrich attitude towards death: we had tidily avoided the subject for so many generations, and suddenly we were being confronted with it every day: and still we weren't ready to believe it wasn't anything but normal. When chaos finally surrounded us: unmanned power stations burning out, imports from abroad not arriving, shops with no staff; petrol stations empty, and riots and panic overtaking everyone's lives, something had to be done. An emergency committee was set up and the current solution was put in place. It hadn't been adopted worldwide: we had to think of our own situation first.

It had taken a while to get used to this way of long-sleeping in a pod, but this method of coping with germs and food shortage had gradually become the norm. Everyone, except the 1st Decades, spent alternate months in a pod: the 0 to 10year olds were carefully nurtured. They were our future.

I looked around at the great towering trees and breathed deeply. The leaves were unfurling, pale green against rust. A brilliant blue sky was the backdrop of dark laced branches that looked close enough to touch. I sighed, fighting back the tears which burned to be free. It was strange and sad to go into the pod when daffodils were poking through, heads bowed in modesty to find, on emergence, that they were sagging damply, brown fingers clutching at their leaves. I missed them. What for me was a blink of an eye in frozen animation was, for them, a lifetime. Maybe plants that spent their winters underground felt the same as I did now.

I turned back to my pod, secured the lock and pressed the sanitising button ready for the next occupant, and then I looked around to see if there was anyone to say 'Hi' to. My skin felt tight after the pod air had worked its magic, and my hair felt soft and downy to the touch: it was shaved once a month for reasons of hygiene, cost, and social equality.

With dragging feet, I wend my way to the register block. Time is running out and I am heartsick at what I must face. Suddenly, I hear my name, the sound sharp to my ears, encased for so long in silence. 'Alicia!' I turn.

'Are you ready?' He looks at me with no expression in his eyes and no smile on his face. He is handsome, tall and powerfully built. I am lucky, I tell myself: he does not repulse me, this partner whom I have been allocated for reproduction. I smile, hoping to see some small flicker of encouragement. I watch his eyes, to see if they will widen even a smidgeon to indicate that he is glad to see me. Nothing. But I know there are feelings there, brooding under the surface.

'I'm ready,' I say.

First, we go to the nursery and feed the children. There are fifty in our unit and I look for my child. Dressed identically in close fitting suits like ours, it is a difficult task. At least the colours are bright and varied, a small concession to joyousness. The food is mush but packed with just the right amount of fibre and minerals and antibiotics to keep us all healthy. It's like feeding time at the zoo, I always think. All these dependent creatures herded together, away from their natural environment and no notion of which of the keepers are their parents.

They are tomorrow's people. And may their god help them to make it a better place; I recognise the sourness in my mind as the thought taints me. I see my child, but I make no special advance to her. I stroke her soft hair and she smiles shyly, like any of them might at a gesture of affection.

Next, we go to the 3rd Decade, the adults. They are busy with various associated tasks, and my companion and I have instructions to check and monitor their performance and capabilities. If they exhibit three consecutive signs of a lack of concentration, or any

83

form of defective behaviour, they are earmarked. These are not physical marks; they are almost worse than that: a secret and ominous black dot against their name. Then they must be demoted to more menial tasks and will not be allowed to reproduce. Some are used for drug experimentation, which is not as bad as it sounds.

We have all been taught to have an altruistic outlook on the purpose of our existence. We must clear the deadwood and keep the human race free of defects, of disease and of lower intelligence, otherwise we will founder, kill each other, and kill the planet. It is this which motivates us: the thought of a better world which we are trying to create. To this end, the 2nd Decade, adolescents, are in training in all the sciences: chemistry, biology, physics, mathematics, biochemistry: there are hundreds of sciences and these are the subjects which are concentrated on.

But today, my heart bleeds. I look at my companion as we make our way back to the children's unit: the 1st Decade. His face remains immobile, all emotions held in check. We stand side by side behind the screen and watch as the controller leads away two children: I see my child again; she is one of the two. Our child. Her illness had been reported earlier and they had allowed me to leave my pod 48 hours sooner than the full 28 days. I had heard the click of the pod unlocking and I knew something was going to be wrong. Today, my daughter will be cryogenically apodised indefinitely, until a cure is found.

At last, the comfort I long for is there, as I feel my companion's fingers curl around mine. I curse the day I was born.

ECHOES FROM THE PAST   by S.F. Formi

The day was gentling to its close. Only the soft rustling of the roosting birds disturbed the peace. I smoked the last of my cigarette as from the house came the call of the gong; supper was ready. I began to make my way across the landscaped grounds. As I did so a chill wind got up, making the bushes tremble. I shivered: of a sudden the atmosphere seemed to have changed.

Then a strange silence fell upon the place. I quickened my step as the evening light played across the garden, casting shadows and creating false images. Or so I thought. But what was this before me? I came to a halt, my skin prickling at the materialisation of something that my logical brain could not define.

It bore the shape of a woman but so ethereal and other worldly that I could not be exactly sure what it was. Wispy wraiths curled from the head. Medusa's snakes sprang to my mind. These trailed down the greyish-white outline and swam sideways at angles.

A great paralysis overtook me, and I remained, as a stone pillar, stuck fast to the ground. My blood ceased to flow; my breath too seemed frozen in my chest. I struggled to recover my senses and a great gasp left me. As I stood there, unable to move, the thing, woman, whatever it was, seemed to elevate and in front of my eyes floated... floated across the lawn and through the tangle of roses and away, until it was no longer visible. I strained my eyes to see what was no longer to be seen. My breath still rasped in my chest but by a huge effort of will, and against all my instincts, I forced my limbs to move, and ran in the direction the apparition had taken.

But then I came to a halt. It was now dusk, and already a light whisper of grey mist was descending over the garden, affording any ghostly creature perfect cover. The being had gone. There was no trace of it: no disturbance on the grass, no thread of white cloth on the rose thorns. Had I imagined it? Suddenly a great wave of exhaustion overtook me and my knees began to tremble. With some difficulty I made my way indoors.

I felt what I had seen must have been some sort of mental aberration and it was not something I could speak of. As a consequence, I was poor company. I was spending the weekend in this ancient house, recently brought back to life by my hosts. Despite their many renovations, the building clung on to the old sounds and sighs of yore; each time there was a creak in the timbers, or a feather of draught touched my person, my head swivelled and my nerves jangled.

'What's with you man?' my old friend Pete demanded.

I shook my head, 'A chill coming on, no more than that.'

'Here,' he said, thumping a glass of neat Glenfiddich beside me, 'get that down you and you'll be right as rain.'

Many more tots of liquor followed that first one. I swallowed them all in an attempt at forgetting that earlier vision. There were four of us: Peter, his wife Ellen, and Robbie, a new acquaintance of Pete's. My friends tried to chivvy me out of what they called 'the doldrums' but without success: I retired to bed early, hoping to escape into oblivion.

It was a troubled night; scattered snatches of sleep were interspersed with odd noises from the house. Towards dawn I was woken by a flickering light dancing through the chink in the curtains. I lay for a moment, the covers drawn up to my chin, as I tried to clear the muzziness from my head. I assumed that the flashing light was something to do with the monstrous migraine that sat like a boulder on my forehead. After a moment or two I realised that was not the case. Slowly I disentangled myself from the muddle of bedclothes and made my way to the window.

As I stretched out a hand to draw back the heavy drape, a banshee like noise hit my ears. I jumped back in dread, sensation after sensation seizing hold of my body as an icy chill crept up my spine until it reached my head, causing my hair to stand on end. My manliness forsaking me, I let out a scream at the sight confronting me. It was the same apparition I had seen in the garden; the figure, approached closer as I stumbled back further into the room, putting out my hands to ward it off.

'No,' I gasped, 'keep away.'

But the Thing pressed closer and closer until it seemed as if it would smother me. I was struggling to breathe, my nostrils full of a strange smell – a mixture of damp earth and decay. Then, of a sudden it seemed to retreat and before my eyes began to reform into a shape. As I watched in amazement, I saw it resolve itself into the figure of a woman. It was the creature I had seen in the garden.

'Do you not know me, Donald?' the voice was high and breathy as if it too had undergone a frightful experience.

I had fallen onto the bed in my haste to back away and now, my wits completely addled, my mouth dry, I could say nothing.

'I am Peter's wife.'

I shook my head and longed with a great passion to be far away from this dark snare that held me.

'Look man, look at me. I am Peter's wife,' it spoke with ferocity.

'No,' I gasped. 'Ellen is Peter's wife.' I shook my head in the hope of dislodging the sight before me.

A writhing about ensued and the atmosphere was charged with anger.

'You have forgotten me Donald.' The words were hissed directly in my face.

'Fiona,' I breathed and closed my eyes.

When I next looked, the room was empty and calm: no vicious wraith whirled around my head, no unpleasant odours assailed me.

I could not make sense of the strange events but finding myself alone brought a great relief. As soon as the household was awake, I threw myself out of bed; pulling on my clothes, I made haste to get down and join my friends. I needed to be with others.

The smoky smell of sausages and bacon sizzling in the pan, wafted towards me as I entered the kitchen. Ellen was at the big range. She shot me a curious glance.

'You're very white Donald. Are you feeling all right?'

I nodded without looking at her, 'Yes, fine.'

I watched as she cracked eggs into the pan and flipped the bacon over. The domestic warmth of the room was soothing and I felt my tension easing. But I could not escape the weirdness of before. We remained silent a few moments, then as she lifted the plates to the table, I noticed her hands were shaking. I looked into her face then and saw the shadows under her eyes, and the once lustrous red hair was now lank and lifeless.

'What about you?' I said, 'are you OK?'

She sank into a chair and pushed back, sighing. 'Just tired, that's all.' She smiled.

'Do you manage this place on your own?'

'A girl comes in twice a week. I could do with more.'

'It's a big house,' I agreed. 'Does Pete lend a hand?'

She laughed, 'You know Pete.'

Did I? I wondered. Just then we heard the sounds of Peter and Robbie coming down the stairs.

'Hey Donald, is that your attire for the day?'

'I'm not coming on the shoot this time, Pete. I don't hunt now.'

'What's happened to you? Do you not remember the great times we had?'

'I'm more into conservation these days. Sorry but that's how it is.'

Robbie looked to his host and saw the grimace there, then gave a mocking laugh. Peter grunted and fell to his breakfast.

I spent the day wandering the moors with my binoculars. I was glad to escape the macho bantering of Peter and Robbie and I had decided to leave the following day. Peter would not be pleased at the cutting short of my visit but I had had enough. Enough of the strange happenings and, I realised, enough of Peter too. My good friend, my best friend, what had gone wrong? Our friendship had soured and Pete was not the man I'd known and admired.

On my return to the house in the late afternoon, I found Ellen slumped in an armchair by the great fire in the living room. She appeared to be dozing and jerked upright when she heard my footsteps.

'You must be tired,' I said.

'It's the nights,' she said, 'bad dreams...horrible, horrible dreams.' Her face crumpled and I thought she was about to cry. I made to go towards her to offer comfort, but she jumped up, saying she had to see to the dinner as the others would be in shortly.

Dinner was as the previous one had been: loud and with, at times, a coarseness I had not known in Pete before. I noticed Robbie tried hard to keep pace; he was a younger man and I saw something of my old self in him – the almost hero-worship.

The bottles were soon empty and Pete laughingly waved an empty one at his wife.

'Time for another,' he said. 'What have you in the kitchen, Ellen?'

She looked surprised. 'Nothing. Did you ask me to get more wine in?'

'I did that.' He turned a black look on her as he rose to his feet.

'No matter. I'll go down to the cellar.'

A silence greeted this announcement. We all knew what had happened in that cellar.

I don't know why I spoke at that moment, but something impelled me.

'I'll come with you,' I said, 'I've never been down there.'

The cellar door swung open with a creak and a gust of cold, musty air rushed towards us. Standing at the top of a flight of stone steps, I looked down into a dark cavernous place. It gave off an eerily sinister atmosphere; I shuddered. Peter reached for the electric light switch which was placed half-way down. As his arm stretched out, I felt a rush as of something coming behind me; iciness enclosed me.

Then a high-pitched scream reduced me to a violent trembling. I heard the sound of a large object tumbling and tumbling, over and over. My heart thudding, my body shaking, I fumbled around for the light switch.

Peter lay on the cellar floor; already a thin red line was seeping from his head. I was frozen, unable to go to his aid. But then Ellen was there.

'No,' she said, 'not again.'

A white shape was on the stairs. I thought I heard a whisper; the word "justice" floated in the air and then it was gone.

I stayed to help Ellen with the funeral arrangements. I thought her pre-occupation and obvious distress was due to the natural shock and grief at the loss of her husband. But then the morning after the burial, we were alone, and she began to speak.

'I'm grateful you stayed Donald. It's been a help.'

I shrugged, 'No problem. Will you be all right?'

She smiled, 'I think I will now.'

I waited.

'It's been...awful.'

Again, I stayed silent.

'It was if something was persecuting me. I was haunted by dreams about her.'

'Haunted? You mean...?'

'It's ridiculous, isn't it?' she attempted a laugh, 'but that's what it felt like.' She sighed. 'No matter. It's over now.' She gave me a keen look. 'You feel it too, don't you? And you know it wasn't an accident?'

'I don't know what to think.' I ran my fingers through my hair.

'You heard it, Donald. You heard her say "justice."'

I shook my head, 'I don't understand. There's no sense to any of it.'

'I can't help it, I'm afraid. I know almost nothing about Pete's first marriage. I didn't meet him until after Fiona's death. You brought me up here the first time. Do you remember?

90

As if I'd forget, I thought bitterly.

The next day Ellen saw the lawyer. She came back with the news.

'It's a lot clearer now,' she said. 'Fiona was going to divorce him. She'd discovered he was having an affair, not the first it seems.'

She paused to let that sink in. She looked as if a great weight had been removed; her face was alight as it was when I first knew her.

'You think that Peter – murdered her?' I found it hard to say the word.

'Don't you?'

'I can't believe...divorce isn't a reason for murder,' I said, shaking my head.

'It was as far as Peter was concerned. You see, Donald, this house, all this land, belonged to Fiona. Pete would have lost everything if she had divorced him.'

I left soon after that. Ellen had started saying things to the effect that she'd known she'd made a mistake soon after marrying Peter. She took my hand as she said this and looked straight at me. Her meaning was clear but it wasn't the moment for commitment. I had to get away; there was too much emotion: too much that was dark in this place. I needed time to get used to the idea that Peter wasn't the man I'd thought, and I needed to re-assess my own feelings towards Ellen. Who knew, maybe after a while it might be possible for the two of us to restore our relationship. Can you go back, or does the past always come after you?

UTOPIAN DREAM   by P.C.R. Penfold

Alma awoke in the open. She blinked, feeling confused and looked around; she was alone. She had a vague memory that usually when she woke up there was someone lying next to her. She thought perhaps she was still dreaming, although she had never had this feeling of being in the present during a dream: of being there in the moment. She thought she usually remembered dreams after sleeping. This felt different.

She stood up, a bit shakily and took a few steps, then looked back to where she had been lying. There was the impression of her body in the warm, dry grass, and she was again surprised that she felt no ill effects from sleeping on the ground. Slowly, she turned a full 360°. Hills surrounded her: valleys and hills as far as she could see. Her eyes were drawn to the light beyond. It was beautiful, hypnotic, it played to her like a piano concerto. It attracted her with an invisible magnetism. She walked towards it.

There was a plateau at the top and the light was the glow from a pink and golden sky. There were bushes and clumps of trees bearing fruit and nuts, and, like the landscape where she had found herself, there were no walls or hedges, no quilts of cultivated fields. In the distance, sunlight winked on a blue sea.

A man was walking towards her, his hands outstretched in welcome.

'Do I know you?' she said.

'Yes, Alma, don't you remember? Welcome.'

'Welcome to where? Am I dead?'

He smiled. 'Please call me Kenneth and no, you're not dead, you're dreaming.'

'I don't know anyone called Kenneth and this doesn't seem like any ordinary dream. I feel conscious. Normally when people dream, they're swept along, not in control of their speech. This is different.'

'It is different, you're right. Do you remember when you volunteered for a sleep and dream experiment?'

'Yes, yes, I do. Is that what this is?'

'Not exactly. That was a while ago. We ran all the tests and you agreed to continue with this extra experiment. We treated you with some drugs to induce contentment. It was all in the contract you signed.'

'I think you had better explain.'

'Of course, come and sit down.'

'Please, just tell me what's happening to me.'

'For a long time now, people everywhere have suffered sleep and dream deprivation due to anxiety, causing a great deal of pain and misery as well as leading to many psychological illnesses.'

'Yes, I see that. And so?'

'At the laboratory where you came as a volunteer, and I must stress that you did volunteer, we have been engaged in a wonderful way of helping overcome stress. The drugs ensure you have a comfortable, recuperative sleep. You start with a deep sleep, followed by REM sleep as normal, but then, after a few hours you come to a dreamscape, a place of beauty and peace which suits your personality, because you have chosen it. You stay there for several more hours, recharging your batteries. When you wake up, you are refreshed in a way you have never experienced before. Imagine, you have no anxieties, you are in control of your life and you are ready to face any number of life's challenges with renewed vigour.'

'I feel as though my emotions are being stifled, muffled by a pillow. Did I actually give you permission to do this? It doesn't sound ethical.'

'You signed; you were paid, and you were advised of your rights. It's true, neither the method nor the results were spelled out, as it was still in the experimental stage. We have since discovered a better way.'

'How do you fit into my dreams? Why are you here?'

'I'm actually sitting by your bedside in the test centre, talking to you, but you are seeing me in your dreamscape.'

'Am I safe? How do I return?'

'All the indications are that anxiety and stress are drastically reduced when you wake up, which you should do soon. I will leave you now. We have something new for you when you wake up. I'll explain about everything then.'

'But I don't remember feeling stressed before...' but Kenneth had gone. Alma tried to define her feelings. Her mind was calm as she attempted to examine what he had told her. She didn't remember giving her permission for this treatment, it was not the sort of risk she would ever take. She remembered the sleep monitoring, but nothing about mind altering drugs.

Alma couldn't tell whether several hours, days, or possibly just minutes had passed, when she awoke in a hospital bed. Her brain still felt full of pillows. She was wearing pyjamas, which seemed right; in her dream she had been wearing jeans and a jumper. That seemed to confirm that she was in the here and now and she felt relieved by this. She pressed the bell by her side and a nurse came hurrying in, smiling.

'Ah, you've finally woken up. How are we today?' The nurse smiled again.

'We're fine. How long have we been asleep?'

The nurse looked only slightly chastened but carried on smiling. 'A couple of weeks, so more of a coma really.' Another bright smile.

Alma was shocked but kept her cool. Two weeks? Her mind screamed. 'I want to see Kenneth, Doctor Kenneth?'

'He won't be along until tomorrow now; he checks on you every day, isn't that nice?' More smiling.

'Are you on something?' Alma tried to sound interested rather than rude.

'Oh yes, we all are. After the drugs didn't work properly, bringing on a coma, you know, the two of you asleep for weeks –

94

you know, you and your friend – Doctor Kenneth discovered another medication, less powerful, which is introduced into all the mains water. Everyone gets it, admittedly some more than others, and we are sooo not stressed out, not about anything. Isn't it wonderful?'

'You think?'

'Oh, yes, I do,' she enthused, 'I've had two patients who died today, and a little boy was run over by a car and will be crippled for life and I didn't even cry. My mother was diagnosed with dementia, not sure which kind yet, but hey, that's life, isn't it?' She grinned idiotically and patted Alma's bed clothes.

'Did anyone else have the drug that I had? My friend, for instance?'

'Yes, the man you came in with is in the next room.'

'Gary? Is he awake?'

'I'll take a look,'

'Could you ask him to come in and visit me, please?'

'OK.' She was almost skipping as she left, still smiling.

A few minutes later, Gary walked in. 'God! Am I glad to see you! I'm surrounded by nutters!'

Alma patted the bed for him to take a seat. 'You know what's happened, don't you?'

'Not exactly, but everyone's on happy pills or something. It's got to stop. We must get hold of the waterboard, the prime minister, the NHS, I don't know – somebody!' Gary pushed a hand through his hair and looked at her suspiciously. 'You're OK, aren't you?'

Alma nodded. 'A bit fuzzy, but I'm not grinning from ear to ear. And we won't be able to get hold of any of those people you suggest. No-one will listen to us; it's gone too far. We need a plan. How does this sound? How would it be if we went back and lived in our own, sort of joint paradise dreamscape? We could take the drug and go together. What do you think?'

'What, sort of live in our fantasy dream world? D'you think it would work?'

'I can't live here like this; it would drive me up the wall.'

'I think that's a great idea. How do we do it?'

'From what Doctor Kenneth said, we choose an ideal place that suits our personality which our brain sorts out for us. We just have to make sure it's the same place for both of us.'

'How do we ensure that we stay there?'

'We take the drug, we go to sleep, then we're together, in our own dream world. When we're there, we just have to stay awake and not let ourselves sleep. That should be easy as we're already getting our quota of sleep back at the hospital. At the moment, I think they bring us back with more drugs, or we'd be in a coma, from what the nurse said.'

'We can only try. Better than staying here in this madhouse.'

The sun was always shining in the land of their dreams; Gary and Alma were running, holding holds and laughing, eternally young, eternally happy, surrounded by beauty and with not a care in the world. Paradise, with no worries at all. Some might say it wasn't real life, but for Gary and Alma, life in the real world wasn't real either.

When Doctor Kenneth came to check on them later that evening, he found them both in the same bed, wrapped in each other's arms in a deep coma, unable to be brought back. His smile was thoughtful when he read their note. He would certainly put this forward as an experiment with a good outcome. He imagined the accolades, the presentations, the science papers, and his expression became euphoric. He would be remembered for this for a very long time. He told the nurse to take very good care of them and left to write his thesis.

AN IMPERFECT LAWN by P.C.R. Penfold

Gregory was jammed up against the garden fence, held there by the handle of the mower. He wasn't a pretty sight, his tongue lolled out and his face was the same colour as the trampled, dark pink dahlias which surrounded him. He was most definitely dead. The mower was a heavy, old cylinder type: petrol driven with rollers, which Gregory always considered made a very good finish to his weed-free lawn. It now purred quietly at his feet. His hands hung limply by his sides and having released the clutch it had stopped, but not switched off the engine. Given time, the petrol would run out with a sputter and the purring would cease.

Annie, his wife, drove nose first into the open garage, parked and struggled out with two bags of shopping. She headed for the side door of the garage which would lead her round to the back door, where she deposited the bags in the kitchen. It was Greg's day off, a Monday. He worked at the local garage and they were open for six days a week, but each of the staff did a five-day week, taking it in turns to have a day off. Greg liked having Mondays, because when it was a bank holiday, he had a nice long weekend with the Tuesday off as well. Annie worked part-time as a receptionist at the doctors' surgery, which was very handy for making appointments when they needed to. On the whole though, they were both quite healthy.

Usually.

She called out, 'Greg, I'm back. Shall I put the kettle on?' There was, of course, no answer. 'Greg?' Annie shrugged off her jacket, hung it up, put the kettle on and started to put away the shopping. By the time she had finished, the kettle had boiled. 'Greg?' she called out again. She could still hear the mower puttering away quietly. 'Tea or coffee?' she called loudly, as she walked up the garden path, though she had only put out one mug. Instead, she was

97

met by an appalling sight, which chilled her to the marrow. Her hand flew to her mouth and she made an unnatural, guttural sound.

'What has happened to you?'

She looked around wildly, as if someone might suddenly appear and tell her it was all a joke. She peered over the fence into next door's garden.

'John! John! Are you there?'

John was in fact just coming out of his back door with a bag of rubbish.

'What is it? What's the matter?' He dropped the bag and hurried over to the fence; Annie sounded very odd, shouting like that. She pointed, but John had to screw his neck around before he could see what she was trying to show him.

'It's Greg! He's dead,' as her hand flew back to her mouth.

'What happened?' But Annie's response was to shrug and hold out her hands in a gesture that spoke for itself.

'Hold on. I'll come round. I'll bring Jane.'

Annie staggered backwards and then ran to the kitchen sink. She vomited dryly. Jane was beside her by then, guiding her to a chair, while John made coffee, familiar enough with the kitchen and also where the alcohol was. He put a generous slug of whisky into all three cups.

'We'd better call the police,' said Jane, and Annie nodded. 'Shall I do it?' John asked. Annie nodded again, seemingly bereft of words or coherent thoughts.

She listened to his one-sided conversation.

'No, I'm calling for my neighbour. The address is.... It's Gregory Marshall... No, I'm John Baker, from next door. Her husband is dead... In the garden. Well, I suppose an ambulance will be needed but he's definitely dead. No, revival is out of the question. He seems to be impaled by a lawn mower. Yes...it's difficult to explain. Yes, a detective would be a good idea. No, we'll all be here, my wife and I are with her now.'

The conversation continued for several minutes and the ambulance arrived soon after. Jane was making soothing comments, while John had gone to take a closer look at his one-time neighbour. Annie seemed to have shrunk and was not saying anything at all. When the ambulance arrived, there was a sudden burst of energy in the room; the medics were more concerned with Annie than with the body in the garden. They said they had to wait for a pathologist and a detective. They were very kind. Nobody mentioned the word murder.

An hour or so later, and the house was still full of people. Annie was feeling very unreal, as if she were an onlooker at a theatre performance. Faces loomed in front of her, enquiring anxiously if she was all right. It was hard to gather her wits enough to provide an answer, so she nodded and attempted a smile. Of course, she wasn't all right! What a stupid question, she thought. Seeing Greg like that…it felt like a play unfolding. After that, events seemed to unfold in slow motion. She watched them take away her husband's body, thoughtfully now covered up. She was glad of that, because the sight of him again may have brought on another desire to vomit, which was uncomfortable on an empty stomach. More time slipped by and a female police officer led her into the sitting room and then, despite her gentle manner, bombarded her with questions.

These seemed irrelevant to Annie, but she coped. How long had they been married? What sort of question was that! Gradually, they changed, becoming more specific. Was the front door unlocked when she came home? Yes, it was, they left it on the latch when they were home. Likewise, the garage doors were open to receive her. The side door of the garage? Yes, that too, would have been unlocked. Her husband was in, after all. Had her husband any enemies? She had to resist the urge to laugh at this point. Instead, she said,

'Why? Hadn't he tripped or something? Wasn't it an accident?'

The mower chose that moment to expire with a sudden burst of clattering engine parts.

This time it was the officer who looked disbelievingly at her. 'Annie, the mower doesn't have a reverse gear, nor was there anything over which he could have tripped. The crossbar of the mower had been forcibly thrust against him, causing his probable death by strangulation. Naturally, we will know more after the post-mortem. I'm sorry, but these are suspicious circumstances. Now, where were we?'

And so it went on. It was getting dark when they all finally left, and that felt just as unreal as the whole of that day: being alone after such momentous happenings, then left with no one to talk to. She knew she should have expected that.

Annie turned on the radio and found some light music and forced herself to eat a piece of toast and thought about who she ought to be phoning, to tell them the awful news. The thought of constantly having to repeat the same dreadful story made her feel quite ill.

Chapter Two

Of course, Gregory had a past. His though, was a little more complex than most. He had always been in the garage business, the one he worked at now was a privately owned one and the owner was an unknown businessman who had employed a manager to run it for him. It became evident, soon after Greg's death that this was a man trading under the name of Barry White. Greg had always been quite a fan, and this was his chosen pseudonym, because it was Greg who owned the garage. The solicitor who sat in front of Annie, who was desperately trying to hold it all together, had a lot of papers on his desk. It seemed that every sheaf of clipped together papers represented a new surprise.

'These,' he said, holding up another bundle, are the deeds of a villa in Capri.'

'Yes, we regularly went on holiday there, but, really, Mr Fitzgerald, we didn't own it! That's ridiculous. Do you mean it was some kind of timeshare?'

Mr Fitzgerald ignored Annie's remark.

'These,' he said, picking up another bundle, 'are the deeds of a villa in Portugal. Quite a large one by the look of the cost.'

'Oh, yes, we went there every year, but you must be mistaken, it was owned by the Reeds who we always went with.'

'Not so. Barry White again. And these,' another substantial bundle was waved at her, 'are for a row of mews flats in London. They are rented out and the maintenance company who owns and runs the business is owned by – guess who? Yes, Barry White. Your husband. He has several bank accounts; he was a very rich man.'

'But…we live in a, well, a very nice, semidetached house in Eltham! He would have told me if he was rich!'

'Would he? And how come he *was* so rich, Mrs Marshall? Do you know that?'

'I didn't *know* he was rich. Isn't that obvious?'

'I'm afraid all of this has got to be handed over to the police. The Inland Revenue will also be interested I believe, but mostly, the Criminal Investigation Team. You do realise that this opens up a great many issues connected to his murder?'

Annie felt faint. The solicitor's voice reached her through a physical haze in the air. 'How long have you been married, Mrs Marshall?'

'What? The police asked me that as well. Why do you want to know?'

'I believe your husband was using your present lifestyle as a cover for err… past, err… indiscretions.'

'By err… past, you mean before he married me?' Annie unconsciously mirrored his speech.

Mr Fitzgerald eagerly leapt on her correct assumption. 'Exactly. I believe he has run his businesses in a perfectly legal fashion over these last few years. Maybe not so legally in the past… how did he make all this money? That is the question; one which I am driven to enquire into, as he seems to have kept it secret from you and from his work colleagues and his neighbours!' Mr Fitzgerald said this with an air of triumph, one which Annie did not share.

'So, what happens now? Is all this money to be confiscated?' Anxiety made her sound aggressive.

'Really, Mrs Marshall, we're just doing our job here! The funeral costs will come out of his current bank accounts, especially as these are in your joint names. Not Mr White's,' he added, with overtones of apology in his voice.

Annie didn't feel she could take any more. She scooped up her bag and pushed back her chair.

'Ten years, Mr Fitzgerald. That's how long. Ten years we were married. Apparently, a lot can be concealed in that time. And another thing: should I be afraid of someone coming into my garden in order to murder me as well?'

Mr Fitzgerald hastily scraped back his own chair. He had temporarily forgotten that Annie Marshall was a bereaved wife and not the recipient of any kind of good news. 'I'm sure the police will take care of you, Mrs Marshall. And please be assured that current expenses can be put through my office if you encounter any kind of cash flow problem.' He stuck out his hand but Annie was already over by the door. 'Goodbye, Mrs Fitzgerald.'

Annie had been home barely long enough to take off her coat when the doorbell summoned her. Two police officers smiled at her in a manner meant to be reassuring: one male and one female.

'Can we come in?' The WPC said, flashing her card. Annie opened the door wider and stood back to let them pass.

'In here,' she indicated, sounding as tired as she felt. 'Please, no more surprises,' she said.

'Mrs Marshall, Annie, may I call you Annie?' Annie nodded.

'Annie, did you know your husband had been in prison?'

'No! No, I did not! What for?'

'We have reason to believe he had an alias: Barry Brown.'

'Not Barry White? Don't you mean Barry White?'

'That too,' said the constable, smiling wryly.

'You'd better tell me all of it,' said Annie, sitting down and waving at them to do the same.

'He was imprisoned for smuggling. He sold farm machines to poorer countries, but inside the tyres there were stashes of cocaine.

He employed drivers to take the tractors, that's what it was mostly, and they pleaded not guilty, saying they were unaware of the concealed contraband. Payment for these deals was then held in offshore accounts. We believe your husband bought properties with the proceeds. Anyhow, two of the drivers were caught and imprisoned, and one of them was recently released. He was very upset with your husband, Annie, because he blamed him for being the ringleader. Through lies and clever lawyers, he took the brunt of the punishment while your husband did a mere eighteen months and took all the money.'

'Are you telling me this man murdered my husband?'

'It seems highly likely, but we are still following up on our enquiries.'

'Do you know where he is? Am I in danger?'

'Now why would you think that Annie?'

'I don't know. If he's violent... and he might think I was involved...'

'Don't you worry, we're on to him; he confided, well, rather loudly, to a fellow prisoner, bragging about revenge, you know, getting payback. We understand from one of your neighbours that someone had been hanging about outside for several days in a blue Volvo. Did you happen to see that?'

'No, I didn't. A blue Volvo you say? I'm afraid I don't know car makes very well.'

'No? well, never mind. It won't be long now.'

'And the money? My solicitor was telling me that my husband owns several properties, no doubt bought with these ill-gotten gains, as they say – do I have to forfeit that?'

'No, I don't believe you do. He officially paid his debt to society and the way the money was handled, or shall we say, laundered, means it has not been directly traceable to the crime.'

She saw the two policemen to the door and waved them off, hoping not too many neighbours were curtain twitching. She smiled to herself. Blue Volvo indeed! The funeral was less than a week away and as soon as it was over, she and Charlie could at last go and live in Spain, in a villa formerly thought to be owned by the Reeds. His alibi was a hundred percent secure as he had made certain with the 'drinks all round' at the pub, celebrating a win on the horses. Ten years in prison had changed him, but not that much.

And the man who had murdered her husband was already on a plane to the Caribbean, his own particular stash of money safely invested in diamonds and neatly sewn all over his young brides wedding dress. He squeezed her innocent little hand and pointed to the view from his window.

AN EXTRAORDINARY SUMMER'S DAY   S.F. Formi

It was the summer we ended up calling, 'that summer.' A golden end to what was likely to be the last time we would all be together in the same way. Tom, the eldest, was off to university and our close sibling group would inevitably become a bit looser.

Tom had just passed his driving test so we went for a day's picnic in his old banger. Having parked in a clearing, we chased up Oak Tree Hill, our favourite picnic location. As always, the rivalry between us forced us to compete with one another and left us all breathless and laughing by the time we got to the top.

'I did it. I did it,' shouted Janey, the youngest.

'You wish,' said Tom, ruffling her curly mop.

'Actually,' said Jack, 'I think Tom and I were neck and neck this time.' His impish grin dared Tom to disagree.

Tom shrugged but more important matters were at hand. I had been busy unloading the knapsacks, and the gingham tablecloth was now spread with what seemed to be the entire contents of the big larder at home: pork pies, home-cooked ham sandwiches with curls of lettuce peeking out, sausage rolls, hard boiled eggs, plus slabs of fruit cake. Very soon, all that remained were a few crumbs and tiny shreds of greenery decorating the ground. My siblings lay around: their limbs, stained a rusty brown by weeks of sun and weather, fell in relaxed attitudes.

I picked up the picnic plates and empty containers and began to pack away.

'Well done, Sophie,' murmured Tom. 'I'm going to miss your tidying up.'

I felt the blush creep into my cheeks as always with Tom's compliments, even though a part of me knew I should resent being limited to the 'female' role.

But this wasn't the day for political conflict, and I stretched back and with the others, bathed in the late summer glow, absorbing the birdsong and the susurration from the breeze in the nearby trees. It was blissful.

Then: 'What's that noise?' said Jack.

For the moment no-one moved or answered. The buzzing got louder.

Tom sat up, and we all followed. There was nothing to be seen but almost at the same moment our hands moved to our ears. We were being deafened.

We looked at one another.

'A helicopter – somewhere?' said Janey.

The boys shook their heads. By now the sun had disappeared and the sky was rapidly darkening. The beauty of the day was gone, obscured by lowering cloud – and something else.

'Look,' said Janey, pointing towards the distance.
A dark spot on the horizon was moving swiftly in our direction. I felt a
cold chill travel through my body. Glancing at the others, I saw astonishment on their faces. Tom was scrabbling in the grass. What was he doing? I wondered, then realised he was trying to get up. I too, attempted to stand, only to find that my body was pinned to the ground. All four of us were held fast by some invisible force.

Jack managed to say, 'what's happening?' but no-one could answer.

My heart began to thump in an alarming manner and I wanted to cry, but no tears came. Instead, a darkness began to envelope me.

All I can remember of the period that followed was a bumping sensation and knowing I was being carried away. I saw nothing until suddenly discovered that I was in some sort of steel room or container. I was able to look around at that point and could see the others stretched out on boards near me. Dark shadows seemed to be hovering over each one of us, but I was not able to make out anything else.

Later, we found ourselves back on the grass. The weather seemed to have righted itself and once again the sun beamed upon us. We compared notes. None of us was able to say for sure what had happened.

'I can't remember anything,' said Jack, 'it was all shadowy.'

'Did we have some sort of collective dream?' asked Tom.

'Does such a thing exist?' I asked, anxious for him to say 'yes.''

But Tom shook his head, 'Maybe, I don't know. But look we're all OK now. Everything seems to be working, doesn't it?' And to prove his point he raised his arms and jumped up and down.

'Yes, that's true,' said Jack, also flexing his limbs.

We were all silent a moment, then the boys grabbed a ball from the bag and began kicking it around, shouting and laughing at the same time. I looked over at Janey. She was biting her lip, her eyes downcast.

'Janey?' I said.

'I want to go home,' she said.

I called to the boys and we began shrugging on the knapsacks but just then Janey, who had very little to carry or pack up, began to cry.

'What's the matter?' said Tom and we all crowded round her.

'Look,' she said.

Her upper arms were marked with tiny pinpricks in perfect circles, as if something had been stamped into her flesh.

'Could it be some sort of wasp or insect sting?' I asked.

Jack spoke in a soft voice, 'I've got it too.'

Then we discovered we all had the same marks – some on our legs as well, and there were also small red indentations as if a small segment of skin had been scraped away. But none of these strange needle marks or patches caused us any pain.

We went home in silence. Eventually we did tell our parents, who were as puzzled as we were, and insisted we report it. However, when we tried to inform the authorities, our story was dismissed as 'collective hysteria,' the marks on the skin waved away as being self-inflicted.

For a time, I ran around, trying to convince anyone who'd listen about what had happened, but eventually I realised people were beginning to talk about me, calling me mad and deranged. So, I stopped.

Ten years have passed. We rarely speak about that time now. Just occasionally when it's only the four of us, we'll go over it again and show each other the marks that we still carry from that extraordinary summer.

IT'S IN THE BAG   by S.F. Formi

It's a dream. It's got to be: that noise, like a sigh or gasp. But I'm staring at the stark hostel walls, at the humped shapes of the other men. No dream then. I hold my breath and listen: nothing but the snores and whistles of two old fellas in the corner. Just as I start to breathe there it is – a half strangled gurgle. I feel the prickle at the back of my neck, then the movement against my legs. What's that? What's going on? I start to shake.

It's the case, the computer bag I 'rescued' when it came flying out of the crashed car. Stay rational Joe. It must be something vibrating in the case. I didn't check inside – why didn't I? Simple answer – because I wanted to get away from the motorway as quickly as possible. By the time I got to the hostel, I was knackered. Then the shock of what I'd witnessed kicked in: the Mercedes roaring across three lanes of motorway, horns blaring, brakes screaming, the thud when the car flipped onto its roof, the crackle as the windscreen shattered – a terrible tangle of metal and glass, blood puddling on the road. From where I stood, beyond the hard shoulder, I could see the driver's head smashed against the side window – eyes unblinking as they filled with blood. I had to get away.

So even at the hostel I don't think of opening the bag. I don't know why I took it really – usually I stay on the right side of the law. I put it in the bottom of the bed: you can't be too careful in these places. I'd seen things happen – family photos lifted while their owners slept – pathetic, stealing someone else's relatives. But that's what it's like. But now I just want to kick that bag – kick it right back to where it came from. Strangely, my legs won't move – can't get a kick out of them. And then it starts again – first the vibration and then that weird gasp-like sound. My blood starts pounding; I make a huge effort to drag myself out of the bed. I start to move – away from the case. It's so hard but I'm nearly free of it. Then, it's like, hands are pulling me back.

Terror takes over; I want to scream, but nothing comes out. The moaning starts and I know that whatever the thing is, it's got me: I'm going to die. Then there's nothing. But I don't die. And when I wake the other blokes are shifting around, going down for breakfast. I make up my mind fast. I've got to get shot of the bag. I'll hand it in, that's what I'll do. Drop it when no cops around – it'll save getting involved. Return it, civic duty done. Before I do though I'm going to check inside – I've got to see what caused me all that grief last night.

I lock myself in the toilet. At first, I hesitate – it squats there, soft expensive leather, a bit out of place on the chipped tiles. Three zipped compartments- quite weighty – how heavy is a laptop? I did use a computer once upon a time, in another life, but my skills are probably well past their sell by now. I take a breath and run the zip down the main section. The bag falls open, contents spilling all over the floor – bundle after bundle of notes, banknotes. I reel backwards with the shock of it – who carries cash like this around these days? There are plenty of ways to transfer money without ever touching the stuff – even I know that. I try to get a handle on how much is there but whichever part of the brain it is that does the maths – it isn't working today. All I know is that I'm staring at more money than I've had in my lifetime.

Normally nothing would get me out of that place before the big breakfast fry up – it's the best hostel for food that I know – but this is different. Also, paranoia is setting in – I am nervous that someone might get hold of the bag and discover what's inside. So I hit the road again. There's no trouble finding the police station but this one is like Piccadilly Circus, busy desk with uniforms, coppers in and out all the time. So at the end of the day me and the bag are still together.

There's one place I can go: good mates from the old days – they've never turned me away. I can't face sleeping rough tonight and I think I can get to their house. Yes – a house, some time since I stayed in someone's home. But the weather is closing in; the cold is piercing my anorak, going right through to my bones. After a couple of hours, I realise I must find some shelter. The railway arches – it's often the arches. At least there's a bit of a roof, usually. Soon as I get there, I fall asleep but it's not sweet dreams. And then I'm awake again; the noise seems everywhere, the sighing, groaning. Sweating, I try to push the case away but it carries on thumping against my body. I'm trapped. The sounds, the weight on my body increases. I can't breathe, I can't move. Nothing else exists. I'm alone with horror. Again I feel like I'm finished. Then suddenly, it's all over. Panting I sit up: I'm not going to wait for anymore. I run. Luckily the house I'm heading for is not far. I stumble down the lane: sunrise – I usually love this time.

Can't stop to look, nor listen to the birds chorusing, not today. I bang on the door and fall inside when my mate opens up.

'Joe!' he says 'What's wrong old pal? You look – terrible.'

'Can I come in Pete?

Pete and Annie fuss around me. I'm sat in the best armchair, hot drink and something to eat. Pete takes my backpack and the computer case and puts them outside in the lobby. I let the bag go – glad to be away from it, and then I close my eyes.

When I open them again, Pete is there, staring right at me.

'What's going on mate?' he says.

'Nothing – nothing to worry about. Just exhausted.'

'It's more than that. You've been raving while you were asleep. It's not like you.'

I look at them – Pete and Annie, they're the truest friends – my only friends. Many a time they've tried to get me to leave the road and stay with them. I've been tempted: it would be a lovely life, but I can't do it. What they've got is near perfection. I can't add anything to that. But maybe they can help me now.

'It's like this Pete,' I begin. I tell him. Everything: the car crash; stealing the bag and what's in it. Then the other stuff. Pete's looking worried.

'What are you saying? You don't believe...that it's well – haunted – do you?'

I can't look him in the face. 'I don't know what I think. I just know how I felt. It was bloody terrible. I can't go through that again.' I bury my head in my hands. I'm trying not to break down. Annie is standing in the doorway, holding the bag.

'I think we'd better have a good look at this,' she says, bringing it closer.

I feel myself drawing back but she and Pete do the honours – taking the money out, adding it all up. Then Pete sits back: 'There's a lot of dough here,' he says. 'It's got to be handed in.'

'Get rid of it. I never wanted the cash. It's the other business...'

Annie's been going through the case carefully. Now she holds something up.

'Look,' she says. 'I've found this.'

We stare at the silver object.

'It's a memory stick isn't it?' says Pete.

'Yes,' says Annie. 'Let's see what's on it.'

She leads us into the little study. This is where she does her writing – features for magazines, things like that. She slots the stick into the computer.

'Oh it's an audio,' she says.

'Can you play it?' I ask, not knowing if I want to hear it.

'As a matter of fact, I can. I've got a piece of software I use for transcribing the interviews I do. I'll just upload it.'

Pete and I wait. Pete drums his fingers on the chair back. Then suddenly it's coming through: a hesitant, slurred voice.

'I am James Dixon... I want to confess to the murder of my business partner, Robbie Martin.'

Then, some muttering about why he'd done it – personal debts, so he'd cleaned out the company account, intending to skip the country. He describes what he did. It is shocking: the detail of a

112

young man screaming and struggling for life, the strangled last gasps. I shrink into myself as I recognise the same sounds that have been tormenting me. The voice breaks up: sobs and drunken weeping; he can't live with it; Robbie was his best mate – they'd done everything together. Then a scrabble of noise as he reaches to switch the recorder off.

Silence. Then Annie, frowning, says she saw something on the telly about a murder. It might be connected. I let out a great sigh and slump forward, hugging myself: 'I don't understand,' I mutter over and over.

'Maybe there are things we can't understand, Joe. Sometimes you just have to accept.' Annie is patting my back as she speaks.

Pete and I take the bag and contents to the police. They're not too interested in how I'd come by it. After that I go to sleep in the spare room. Nothing grabs me; nothing whispers to me; nothing, just sleep. When I wake, Pete and Annie tell me Kate is coming to supper. I know Kate. I think of her in her quiet cottage and I feel a sort of peace. Last time I saw her there was a question hanging in the air, which I ignored. Now I look over at Annie and see a look of determination as she gazes back at me.

WINCHELSEA BEACH   by S.F. Formi

It's not a tourist spot:
crowds don't throng.
No beach umbrellas or ice cream kiosks.
No raucous shouts of surfing teenagers
or unruly children
to disturb our peace.

Hellos and mornings pass
between walkers, joggers, cyclists
but no intrusion
into endless blue and green.

White shapes dot the marsh
A glint of grey the lake
they swim in.
Their calls reach me
from the distance.
Gulls, terns, ducks, maybe
a little egret.

So does the sea call,
rushing and sucking.
Its rhythm constant, timeless.

Feet scrunch on the shingle.
Stones of many colours, shapes and sizes,
pink and grey, mottled and black.
I cannot resist: my hands
scoop and stroke, trace the shape

worn smooth by the waves,
their sun-kissed warmth seeps into my being.

And with them the miniature worlds of shells,
the once residence of crabs, cuttlefish and cockles,
mussel shells, linked pairs of blue-grey
as if hiding a prize.
Fan-shaped scallop shells,
perfect for decorating a pot.

I finger their delicate edges,
note their pattern, wonder
about their former owners.
Amongst the pebbles are
clumps of sea cabbage, yellow-horned poppy.
The brilliant blue blaze of vipers' bugloss
takes centre stage today.
And something pink creeps here and there.

My walk takes me on – which way to look?
To one side the bird sanctuary with
the mewling sea birds.
To the other, that inescapable giant
that shushes and hushes unceasingly.

This place is no sun-baked paradise.
At times the stinging wind blows faces
red raw.
But it is a place away from sound and fury,
save nature's noise.
There is an atmosphere here
that fills and refreshes me.
Though bounded by sea and sky
yet it makes me feel unbounded.

SINCE YOU'VE BEEN GONE   by P.C.R. Penfold

Derek stood in the middle of the kitchen, waiting for the empty feeling in the pit of his stomach to subside. He looked around, noticing for the first time that the walls needed fresh paint. He had spent yesterday clearing the food cupboards of things he was uncertain either what they were to be used for or were out of date. He realised that since Margaret had died, he had only bought what he had needed that week, whereas she always seemed to have a contingency larder and never ran out of anything.

Of course, their marriage hadn't been roses all the way: she nagged him to clear his shoes from the sitting room and likewise, he nagged her for not putting the milk back in the fridge. They each had their annoying foibles but on the whole, their relationship had been placidly comfortable. But since her death, he had been moping around the house getting more and more depressed. He had let things slip and Margaret would have been quite upset if she saw the mess that was everywhere. He squared his shoulders and said out loud, 'things are going to change; things are going to be different from now on.'

He started by having a shower and putting on fresh clothes instead of the usual gardening things he habitually slouched around the house in. He ate a biscuit and drank a glass of water and then set off to buy paint for the kitchen. It was a start, however small. He walked through to the high street, and fairly swiftly chose a tin of pale grey paint from the hardware shop on the corner. Glancing to his left, he noted the café opposite, where people were already sitting and eating at the tables outside. He asked the shop assistant:

'What's that place like, over the road?'

'Tiffany's? It's great, nice breakfast menu; bit different, you know what I mean?'

116

Derek's stomach felt hollow but he felt sure now that it was through hunger. Still intent on new experiences, he decided this would be a good way to continue. There was a menu board outside listing a great variety of breakfasts: from poached eggs on toast to croissants and coffee. He went in and treated himself to scrambled eggs with smoked salmon and then found a seat outside, clutching the wooden spoon he had been given with a number painted on it. He chose a place that was catching the morning sun and looked around. It was evidently a favourite breakfast venue. It was a good choice, he thought, and looked forward to the novelty of freshly served food cooked by someone else. It seemed like a long time since Margaret had spoiled him; he should have cooked for her occasionally instead of always being the one on the receiving end. He felt guilty that he had not done more for her.

He enjoyed the meal: perfectly cooked and hot and then sat back in the comfortable chair and sipped his coffee. A man in late middle age approached, clutching a cup of something and with a newspaper tucked under his arm.

'This is the only seat left, d'you mind if I join you?'

'No, no that's OK. Help yourself.'

The man set the newspaper down and sat heavily into the chair. He took a few sips of tea. 'Nice here, isn't it? And lovely weather for October.'

'Yes, it is. I've not been here before.'

'I've only been coming here since my dog died. Miss the company, you know.'

'I know what you mean. For me, it was my wife. I miss her too.' Derek did indeed miss more than just Margaret's cooking and her doing most of the housework. He also missed her gentle scolding, and the way they told each other everything, what they were thinking, their opinion of what was on TV or the news, or what they were reading.

'You could get another dog, couldn't you?' he said, whilst also thinking that getting another wife would not be the same.

117

The man echoed his thoughts and put him right on that. 'I'm getting too old to have a young dog and I could never replace old Murphy. Just have to find another interest, I suppose.'

'D'you play bowls?' Where had that come from? Derek wondered; he had never even thought of playing bowls himself. Perhaps the other man might be missing the exercise after losing his dog. He could certainly do with it, and maybe it would provide an interest for him as well.

The other man looked thoughtful. 'No, but I could. D'you know where there is one? You know, a bowling green?'

'Behind the Leisure Centre, I believe. You've finished your tea, I see. Shall we go and take a look?'

'Why not?'

They left money on the table and walked down the high street, chatting like old friends. No one was playing when they got there, but they soon found someone who told them all the details and when they usually met. They even decided on buying the whites they would need from the sportswear shop on site. They booked themselves in for the next session, stressing that they were novices.

'Not a problem,' said the nice lady, 'we all have to start somewhere.'

Derek and his new friend, Mike, shook hands and went their separate ways, promising to meet at Tiffany's before making their way to the Green the following Wednesday.

When Derek got home, he put on the radio and started clearing the kitchen ready for painting. He whistled a tune that he and Margaret used to enjoy by Diana Ross, 'Since you've been gone, I've been missing you.' For once, it didn't make him quite so sad; he had something to look forward to.

The two men met as planned, both carrying their kit bags. They had a coffee first then set off down the high street to the Bowls Centre.

'What did you used to be, Derek?'

'You know, that's what I'm hating most about being retired! What I used to be was a father: before my daughter died of cancer in

118

her forties and my son went to live in Australia, I used to be a husband: before my wife died; and I used to be a buyer for M&S food stores. I'm fed-up with not having an identity! Don't you ever feel that way?'

'Never really thought about it, but you're right. I was in admin for a private hospital, IC of ground staff and maintenance. I was rushed off my feet every day for years, and now, well, it's left a big hole. And you're right, I would like to do something to fill it. Hence the Bowls, right?'

'Yes, but…I want to be someone. I want to be the guy who went to Japan for his holiday, or runs a walking club, I don't know, not just someone who no one even knows, because I never go out!'

'Well, what's stopping you?'

Derek stopped mid stride and looked at his companion. 'Me, I suppose.'

'Exactly. Plan it, organise it. I'm up for it. I've often thought I'd like to run a gardening club, where people could meet every month, maybe in my shed! And we would swap plants, sell things we'd grown, and occasionally go and visit open gardens. I could even organise doing some voluntary gardening for people who are unable to cope, even if only temporarily. What d'you think?'

'I'm up for it. Anyway, we're here now. Let's see what we make of this! But yes, why not? We can talk about it later, after we've learnt how to bowl!'

A year had passed since the two had first met and Derek's bed was strewn with clothes, quite a few of which were new, when the phone rang.

'Hello Derek, how's it going?'

'Nearly ready Mike. Give me ten minutes and I'll be there.'

'OK. I've handed the shed keys over to Lucy. I think I'll be lucky to get them back she's so keen to put her own stamp on the gardener's club.'

'She's great, isn't she? Got your tickets and passport?'

'All set. Japan and Australia, here we come!'

119

PAYBACK   by P.C.R. Penfold

There had been six of them seated around the table; poetry books and papers fluttered beside coffee cups and plates with crumbs, remnants of the delicious biscuits Sherry had made. The meeting had gone well. Sherry always felt uplifted by the poems they all chose and then read out loud. Some of their number also wrote poems which were then critiqued by Tod. He was the only man and by dint of also being the only professional (he was a former literature teacher) felt it his duty to pass the strongest of opinions and detailed explanations of each poem. No one seemed to mind, as he also sent out all the emails to say where and when the next meeting would be held, and always brought along some interesting poems which he had studied and researched in depth and could then impress them all with his knowledge.

It was 6 o'clock and they had all left; Sherry had taken that day's dinner out of the fridge ready to heat up. They had eaten cottage pie the day before and what was left of the meat she had put on one side for today and was now adding tomatoes and herbs to make a Bolognese sauce. All she had to do then was cook some spaghetti.

Dan had come home from work and they had enjoyed a pre-dinner gin and tonic while talking over their day. They had just finished eating and were intending to relax in front of the television when the telephone rang.

It was Sophie: 'Sherry, I can't find my ring! I must have lost it at your place this afternoon, would you be a dear and have a look for it?'

'I think I would have seen it when I cleared the table. Are you sure you lost it here?'

'Yes. Absolutely. The thing is, it gets a bit loose when my hands are cold, and well, your house wasn't very warm this afternoon, was it!'

'I'm sorry, I didn't notice, you should have said! I could have turned the heating up.'

'Please Sherry, would you just go and look and then call me back? I shan't sleep tonight if you don't find it.'

'Well, yes, I will, but have you checked you didn't lose it in the car? Or after you got home?'

'Of course I have! You have to look, now! I shall have to report it to the police as stolen if you don't find it.'

'You can't do that! Not if you've lost it!'

'That ring is worth a lot of money. I really don't have a choice.'

Sherry put the phone back and told Dan what Sophie had said. They had a look on the carpet near the table and Dan even tipped up the settee to see if it had rolled underneath it.

'Why don't you phone the others and see if they remember seeing her wearing it?'

Sherry thought that was a good idea and started with her friend Liz. She was genuinely shocked that Sophie had talked about calling the police.

'That sounds very threatening, doesn't it? Like she thinks we stole it? The police would be all over us, as if we were criminals!'

Sherry then phoned Tod. 'Not the sort of thing I notice I'm afraid. Bit daft wearing it if it's worth all that. She should get it made smaller.'

Sherry agreed. Then she phoned Tess, but she had to leave a message as no one answered. She thought about ringing her mobile but decided against it. Tess had been cosying up to Tod all afternoon and was unlikely to have noticed anyone else in the room. That just left Kirsty. Sherry checked the time: it was now 10 o'clock and she was quite sure that Kirsty would be in bed and not at all happy at being phoned about Sophie's expensive ring. She decided to leave it until the morning, but thought she had better phone Sophie back.

'No luck, I'm afraid and no one actually remembers you wearing it. It must be in the car, or in your bathroom or something. Sorry!'

Sophie spoke sharply: 'Look again! I have turned my house upside down and inside out, and the car as well. I will definitely be calling the police.'

Sherry had no intention of renewing her search, for reasons she did not wish to share at that moment, but replied sweetly: 'You said yourself it was loose, the police aren't going to help you find a lost ring, are they?'

'Well! I'm going to have to look into it, find out what I need to say to the insurance company.'

Sherry made reassuring noises which she hoped did not sound too insincere.

Sophie's husband was furious. He had told her not to wear it, it was too valuable. 'But you have it insured, don't you?' Sophie whined. Paul grunted and was obviously angry with her, so she decided to keep out of his way. She went to bed without saying goodnight but lay trying to think when she had last seen the ring. It wasn't on her dressing table or in the bathroom, and she was certain she had put it on that morning. After that she really couldn't be sure. She knew from experience that it could easily slip from her finger and it was sometimes ages before she noticed its absence.

She began to feel rather guilty. She liked to wear it to show her friends that they had money, even though Paul said she mustn't. When she asked him why not, he had said it was an investment and the money might one day come in handy. She was aware that it wasn't new, after all, it had not been made to fit her and that was why it was loose. She had asked Paul to have it made smaller but he seemed unwilling. He said something about losing the gold hallmark which would devalue it. She was beginning to suspect that he had not actually got around to insuring it at all. She dared not remind him about it, his temper was unpredictable and she still had the bruises to prove it. Not that she had ever told anyone about that.

Not a soul. She was loyal to Paul: he was a good catch, and he was never short of cash.

Meanwhile, Sherry phoned Tess again, guessing she had not picked up her message, and received the answer she was expecting. 'Sorry, haven't a clue. Serves her right. She shouldn't have been flashing it around.'

'But did you notice if she was wearing it yesterday?'

'No. I've seen it once or twice but don't recall seeing it yesterday. Sorry, got to dash. Bye.'

Next, she phoned Kirsty. Kirsty was an ex-policewoman, though not everyone knew that.

'What would happen if Sophie reported her ring as lost, to the police?' Sherry asked.

Kirsty was cautious, as ever. 'She'd be lying if she told them it was stolen. No sign of a break-in etc. I'm not sure where they stand with lost property, even if it is valuable. They really are too busy to worry about things like that. The most that they're likely to do is ask her for a photo of it so they can check it against recovered stolen jewellery. I somehow don't see Paul letting that happen, do you?'

'No, and she doesn't know my brother John, is a jeweller. I don't think they were living here three years ago when my dad's shop was robbed. And the other thing she doesn't know is that I described the ring to John and he was quite convinced it was one of theirs.'

'Hmm. That would make telling the police a bit of a problem wouldn't it. Same thing with insurance. Obviously, she doesn't know does she.'

'That her husband is a thief? Evidently not. He has apparently gone ballistic that she's been wearing it. Serves them right.'

Sherry's next call was to John. 'Do you want to call in for coffee later?' She fished in her pocket and held the ring up to the light, admiring its brilliance and clarity. 'I have something for you, a return of lost property, you might say.'

MEANT TO MEET   by P.C.R. Penfold

Until a few weeks ago, Elinor, or Eli as she preferred to be called, had an unremarkable life. She was twenty-seven, lived at home with her parents but this did not curtail her freedom, so not as bad as it sounds. She had a well-paid position as a negotiator with an insurance company, and she enjoyed it. She did not have a boyfriend, but that was all right because she was saving to buy a flat. She looked forward to a bit of independence. Boyfriends always wanted to do things that cost money and then wanted you to go halves, even when it was something you didn't particularly want to do in the first place. When the time was right, she felt confident that she would meet someone who was more on her wavelength.

She awoke one morning to the sound of a noisy exhaust hurtling up the road at a speed which was definitely exceeding the 40mph specified. The unexpected disturbance caught her mid-dream. She lay still, keeping her eyes closed and tried to remember the details of it, but they slipped back into the recesses of her mind, elusive as a butterfly that flies away as soon as you want to look more closely. She vaguely remembered being in a large room or maybe it was a barn, with a lot of antique furniture, and there was a man there too, but she couldn't recall him clearly, and nor did she recognise him. She saw only a back view: tall and quite thin with dark, curly hair. She gave up trying to recall any more and instead, went to work earlier than usual.

A few days later, she woke up feeling she had dreamed about the same man and the same barn again, only this time, she had browsed through the furniture, ornaments and pictures and spoken to the tall man. He was rather handsome and very friendly, helping her to choose something to buy. She didn't know what that might be but she was always interested in bric-a-brac, hoping one day to find a priceless treasure that no-one else had spotted. As if!

Later that day, there was a meeting at work. By the time it ended it was after 5pm and not worth starting anything fresh, so she opted to go home early. She walked through the back roads to her car, where her attention was caught by a single yellow flyer tucked under the windscreen wiper. It announced a barn sale of furniture and collectables at an address which she vaguely knew. She checked her watch and saw that it was still open. It might be interesting, the word 'barn' having caught her attention. She could do with a bookcase for her room and also a chair: something small and comfortable.

On arrival, she saw that the barn was like the one in her dream: old, large, and filled with shelves and furniture pieces as well as general bric-a-brac. Not surprising she thought, after all, it was just a barn. Lights were being switched off and she took the hint and left after a quick look around on the off chance of seeing if a tall, thin man might appear. She smiled at her own attempt at serendipity when he didn't, then drove home with a promise to herself to go back in a few days, when it wasn't just about to close.

A few days later, she awoke feeling muzzy headed. She tried to figure out what had caused her to wake up, but there was nothing she could pin it to, other than the crazy motorist. She filtered through her mind to capture the remnants of her dream. It was as elusive as ever, but later, seeing their two cats in the kitchen, both sitting and meowing for their breakfast, brought back a fragment of it. She recalled an image of Leo stuck in a tree in the garden, and Gem climbing up next to him, resulting in two cats being stuck up the tree. The tall young man from the barn shop happened to stop by and helped her with a ladder to rescue them. She smiled and thought about how odd dreams could be.

She went to work as usual, but all day she mused on the subject of her dreams and concluded she must need a knight in armour, subconsciously, of course. On her way home, she decided to go and look around the barn again, to see if they had a bookcase.

The long barn, packed with tables, was full of shadows: memories were alive everywhere in the pre-owned items from long ago. She felt herself enveloped by them. Hearing footsteps, she glanced up and there was the tall thin man, walking towards her. His arms were outstretched and his look of astonishment was almost comical. Even though she recognised him from her dream, she faltered at his apparent recognition of her.

'Do I know you?' she asked as he stood in front of her.

'Oh, I'm so sorry! I couldn't help it.' He was still staring at her, but now, more in puzzlement. 'Please, come with me.'

He grabbed her hand and was half dragging her between the stalls to the far end of the barn, where there was an area sectioned off to form an office with windows, through which she could see someone was sitting at a desk.

'You have to meet my father. I have something to show you.'

Eli had not spoken, and her initial discomfort was swiftly being replaced with curiosity. Her companion burst through the door and made a theatrical display with his arm to both his father and also, to the portrait on the wall above his head. She stared. The painting was the side view of a young woman seated, ankles crossed, her hands folded in her lap. She was looking at the artist, which translated itself to eye contact with anyone who looked at the painting. Eli was immediately drawn in, but strangely felt she was looking at herself in a mirror. How could that be?

The older man was gawping at her, in a similar manner to that of his son. Eli started to feel uncomfortable. 'Who is that?' She pointed at the picture.

'My wife. She died in childbirth. 29th May 1984. A date that's engraved on my heart.' His voice wobbled and he looked embarrassingly close to tears.

'That's my birthday.'

'I rather thought it might be. You'd better sit down.' She did so and waited for him to explain.

126

'Did you know you were adopted?' The older man looked as shocked as she felt and asked the question quietly. He seemed driven by an unstoppable force, unable to say it any other way, no matter how stark it sounded. He sighed with relief at her answer.

'Yes. Yes, I did, they always told me, it was never a secret. But… are *you* my father?'

'Yes, I am. I hope you have been happy?

'Yes, of course, they were, and still are wonderful people.'

'I hope you will forgive me – let me tell you about it.'

'I was in the Army and I had a posting overseas. I was distraught at my wife's death and didn't get back in time. I will admit, I did not handle it well. I couldn't bear to keep you and…well… it seemed impossible at the time.'

Eli was shocked and looked as if she might faint. Gary, her half-brother, had opened some brandy and found glasses from one of the stalls. They all sipped the strong, revitalising liquor, silently wrapped in memories and private reflections. Her father continued.

'I put you out of my mind. The adopting agency was a good one, and I knew I could never look after you like a proper family could. I hope you understand that. For many years I have prayed for my wife's forgiveness in giving away her child: a daughter whom she would have loved and who she gave up her life for.'

He leaned back in his chair and his chin dropped heavily. 'For me though, it was different. I couldn't look at you without knowing you were the reason for her death.' He sighed, heavily. 'Gary here knows – I told him everything. He said he would find you, that I was missing out. That he and you both deserved to know the truth. I see now that blaming you was unfair, although I hope that ultimately, I did the right thing and you found happiness with your new family.'

Eli nodded; she felt too emotional, and too shocked to speak. It was a lot to take in on a Wednesday afternoon. She looked up at them both and saw only kindness and a desire for her forgiveness. Several minutes passed before she trusted herself to say anything.

'I think we were meant to meet. You see, I had a dream.'

THE SPACE IN BETWEEN   by S.F. Formi

It was growing dark and my attempts to jolly myself out of my anxiety had all dissipated into the gloom around me. I was afraid: I had no idea what to do, which way to turn. It had been a beautiful clear day when we'd set off and yes, of course, I knew that the weather in the Lakes could change dramatically in a short space of time. But then I had no thought that I would become separated from the main party. How had that happened?

I couldn't help a nagging feeling that it was to do with that issue Simon had chosen to resurrect. Why did he have to start that stupid quarrel all over again? Hadn't we dealt with that? Hadn't we agreed? I would take the offered promotion and he would drop down to a part-time role. I wondered what had gone wrong between us but then caught myself in mid-thought; this would get me nowhere. Right now, my focus must be on my current situation.

The mist was getting thicker. It felt like I was becoming wrapped in a blanket restricting all movement and preventing me from seeing any possible landmarks. I pulled my anorak closer and edged into the lee of the mountain. If I didn't find some shelter before nightfall, I knew I could be in real trouble. From my rucksack I pulled out my pink jumper and a groundsheet. Settling myself into a crevice in the rock I determined to concentrate on making a plan; the trouble was my mind was darting everywhere and I seemed unable to think straight. One minute I was seeing Simon laughing with the others in the walking party just before I became lost; then there was a memory of him saying he'd dropped his torch – it was just behind me, would I pick it up? But it wasn't. I couldn't find it and when I looked round, I was alone. Then I had the image of a stretcher with a covered body being carried down the mountain. I shook my head: that wasn't going to happen to me, but my brain hurt and was as fog-bound as my body.

Then I remembered the emergency rations. The hot chocolate warmed me enough to give me some hope but soon tiredness began to overtake me. My eyelids started to droop. A noise brought me to – what was that? In this eerily silent world, any sound was significant. There it was again – a soft padding and then a snuffle. My body froze but my imagination went into overdrive – a creature of some sort and close by.

There was nothing I could do, nowhere to run. The sounds came closer, then out of the mist came a long muzzle, followed by two pointed ears and the keen eyes of a wolf. My heart pounded – I had no weapon, no means of escape. The wolf put its head on one side, then the other as it examined me. It whined. I held my breath.

'Hello,' I whispered. 'Good boy.' The words came out in a croak.

'Well now,' said the wolf, 'you're in a bit of a pickle I must say.'

I blinked – had I heard that? I must be delusional.

'What are you doing out here in this weather? Don't you know the mountain is a dangerous place to be?

My tongue seemed stuck to the roof of my mouth: I could not speak. The wolf came closer. He sat down in front of me and crossed his paws as if settling down to read a good book.

'Perhaps I should introduce myself,' he said. 'My name's Hero.' He paused, 'good name, eh? Actually, it's a bit of a joke amongst the pack because I'm really a bit of a wimp.'

If it's possible for a wolf to look sheepish then I have to say that is what happened at that moment. I continued to stare dumbfounded and mesmerised.

'Cat got your tongue?' he said. 'Come on, what's your name? I do hope it's not 'arold or T'elma. I have trouble pronouncing the aitch and the tee-aitch.'

'It's Liz,' I said.

'Good. I can manage that. So now, Liz, tell me all about it.' His ears twitched and his eyes, those strange grey-white eyes that wolves have, seemed to look into my very being.

'About what?' I gulped and looked around. This couldn't be real. Here I was talking to a wolf. I tried to edge back a little but my spine was already touching rock.

'About how you came to be here,' he said this slowly as if speaking to a child. 'What is wrong in your life that you end up in this situation?'

'Nothing. Why should anything be wrong? I just got lost, separated from the group – that's all.'

'Hmm,' a paw stroked his jaw as he studied me. 'In my experience there's usually more to it.'

'What, what do you mean?'

'It is sometimes the case that the situations we find ourselves in are brought about by some need, possibly sub-conscious, to bring something to a head, or just to give us time to ourselves, time to think.'

I stared at him. A wolf psychoanalyst? I must have gone mad, off my head. They'd find me in the morning running in circles and babbling.

'I see that you are finding all this difficult to absorb. I suggest you try and suspend your logical human brain for a moment.'

I said nothing and Hero continued: 'The alternative theory to the one just given is that someone else, that is to say A.N. Other, wished to cause an event such as has happened to you. This may be for their own reasons – we can speculate that those reasons may not be for the good of the individual involved – may in fact result in harm to the person affected. But again, it may be that this other merely wished to gain some distance from a scenario he, or she, is finding troubling,   as   in   my   earlier   suggestion.'

The thought wormed its way into my head: had Simon intended that I should get 'lost'? The idea was unthinkable, wasn't it?

The wolf watched me for a moment as I tried to take all this into my confused and spinning brain. Then he began a slow grooming of his coat, his eyes flicking up to my face at intervals. I was fascinated, unable to take my gaze from the movement of the long pink tongue snaking in and out of his mouth, the dagger-like teeth nibbling at his fur.

Grooming ceased, he returned full attention to me. 'People sometimes say something like "I need to feel at peace with myself"'. He nodded as if to reinforce what he'd said. 'Space,' he said 'between actions, but also between words, between being. A lacuna of sorts you might say, in which the individual may be restored, may recover their balance.'

There was a silence. Hero yawned, stretched, then looked around him and sniffed first the ground and then the air. 'It is getting late. You will not be found tonight.' He reached out a paw to me. 'If you permit me, I will keep you warm this night and you will be safe.'

I nodded, unable to speak. He crept up to me, snuggling his body around mine, his bushy tail wrapping itself across my legs. His head was on my shoulder; I could feel his hot breath on my neck. It smelt of raw meat and something else – something wild and free, and strong. His ears twitched in my hair. I slept.

The morning sun woke me. The day was clear and sparkling, the landscape smiling and serene as if nothing strange or dark could ever happen here. I heard a shout and a scrabble of feet and there they were – my rescuers. Simon was running behind the professionals; he was out of breath and tears were pouring down his face.

'Liz, I thought I'd lost you,' he said as he got closer to me. 'It's all my fault. I'm so sorry, sorry.' He pulled me into his arms but one of the men disentangled me saying I must be wrapped in the foil blanket in case of hypothermia. As he made to do this, he held up a clump of greyish-black fur. 'Hello,' he said, 'what's this? Have you had visitors?'

I laughed and took the fur from his hand, stuffing it in my pocket. 'Oh, it's the spare jumper I had. It moults all the time.'

Simon had a strange look on his face 'You don't have...' then stopped.

131

As the rescue team made their arrangements for descent, he sat by me.

'Liz,' he said. He reached for my hand in the aluminium wrap, 'you are all right, aren't you?'

The memory returned; the feeling of having been abandoned, deliberately?

I shivered and pulled away; the paramedic tightened the silver covering. I was cocooned, a shiny chrysalis; perhaps a new me would emerge.

'I've been thinking,' I said, 'I think we both need some space. Some time for reflection.'

Simon's gaze slid away from my eyes.

CARPE DIEM   by P.C.R. Penfold

The last stars hesitantly kiss the night goodbye.

The moon, fragile and ghostly, lingers on, reluctant to leave.

An owl glides silently past, eager to be home to her family

And small creatures shiver, glad to be alive.

She turns, cool mist stroking her skin, frost crystals biting her toes

and lifts up her arms as if she would raise up the sun,

and invisibly, it infuses the sky with soft warmth.

She embraces and seizes the day whispering:

'I love you. I will love you forever.'

CHANCES   by P.C.R. Penfold

Linda stroked the blonde curls from her daughter's soft round cheek and kissed her as she lay sleeping. Not for the first time she felt a pang of gratitude to her grandfather. She tucked Maisie's favourite rabbit under the duvet, carefully resting its floppy blue ears on the pillow

When she thought about her and Paul's time together, she knew that nothing had ever challenged their relationship as much as her pregnancy: no hint of tragedy or upset had ever happened to stop them from just having a good time. He was always up for anything, the more bizarre and impromptu, the better. She had enjoyed that. They were always taking weekend breaks, skiing, ballooning, going to shows or parties; life was full of fun and settling down was never part of the picture. Until she became pregnant. This was after a bout of sickness which caused the contraceptive pill to fail.

Paul had given her money for an abortion, no discussion, he just could not face it, and then he had dropped her, cleared out of her life without a backward glance. When she said she needed to think about it: that abortion was not something she wanted, he said he was not prepared to have a child under any circumstances; settling down with a family was not for him and he had stormed out of her life. Thank goodness her grandfather's voice of reason had saved her: saved them both. He had reminded her that the tiny foetus would already have facial features, a heart that was steadily beating independently of her own. She knew he was right. She couldn't do it.

The shock of his reaction had deeply upset her. He had been a loving boyfriend for two years, each still living with their parents. Her pregnancy had changed all that. She felt foolish, realising that

134

those times together had not been the foundation for a long-term relationship, as they had been for her.

Linda's parents were professional musicians and would never have the time to help her with a baby. They were rarely at home: away on tours or just having fun, like she had been. Then Grandpa had stepped in. Grandma had died two years earlier and Grandpa had said he was glad to be of use. He said he would help her to look after the baby and support her in every way he could and to make it easier, she could come and live with him. She did not need much persuading. It was not the best solution, where Maisie could have grown up knowing her father, because that was clearly not going to happen. She had taken up her grandfather's offer and had never regretted it in the four years since.

Even with Grandpa's help, looking after Maisie as a single mum had its problems. He helped her financially, and with minding Maisie now she was back at work, and she didn't know how she would have coped without him. She thought about him with affection, thinking the word that best summed him up, was 'comfortable.' He wore corduroys and cardigans, and she could understand the warm glow that Maisie showed when she wrapped her little arms around his legs. He was always quiet, always reasonable and both Linda and Maisie adored him.

Linda closed Maisie's bedroom door and went to change. She was meeting a colleague from the magazine where she worked, for a drink. She had a regular column that featured a different-up-and-coming talent every month and Russell was one of the co-editors. She liked him; he was easy to talk to although their conversation was nearly always about a project they were chasing, or sometimes someone else's on the team. It was good to be able to discuss things before submitting them to the editor. He often came with her to the gigs she had to attend, and vice versa, and his opinions helped her assess the angle she would take in her articles. She liked to keep it interesting, with a bit of gossip and some personal stuff that the readers could identify with. These were not highflyers: it was only the mega stars who earned huge amounts of money and 'lived the dream' and who had mostly lost sight of their humble origins. Her talent-spotting was a bit more down to earth than that: they were essentially true-life low-key success stories.

Russell greeted her with a peck on the cheek. 'How's the infant?'

'She's fine, my grandfather is in charge, so couldn't be better.'

'He's pretty useful, isn't he? Unpaid helper and all that?'

Linda felt herself bristle hearing him describing her favourite relative in that way.

'He's happy to do it. He doesn't need money, and nor would he take it if he did.'

'Easy! I didn't mean anything by it. Just that some people aren't so lucky are they.'

'No, I suppose not. But money has never been an issue. I'm sorry, and maybe I do take him a tad for granted.'

'Are your parents in the picture as well?'

'My parents are very much immersed in their own careers. They both play professionally: oboe and clarinet in a national orchestra. We barely see them, what with travelling and all that. Anyway, enough with the inquisition! My turn now! How about you? Have you decided to move in with Emma yet?'

'Yes and no. I wouldn't mind us living together but not in her place. It's too small for my liking: no room for my cat, no room for my motor bike, no room for my books. And she doesn't want to live in my flat. Too far from her job. Anyway, I'm moving back home this weekend, to save money. Unfortunately, that means putting up with my mentally deficient younger brother.'

'That bad, eh? Why don't you buy a place together that suits you both? Save while you're with the parents.'

'We don't all come from affluent homes like you. No inheritance on the horizon and Emma's job at the dog parlour doesn't pay well. I told her she should try for a veterinary nurse: get herself a qualification. We both need a rise before we can save anything.'

'I know. Property prices are a nightmare. So: good plan: you can save up.'

'Hmm. Doesn't solve the problem of the annoying brother. Drink?'

'I'll get these since you're so poor. Shall I get a bottle of house red and we can share? Crisps?'

'Great, but no crisps thanks.'

They drank slowly and the talk returned to gigs, and the struggle some of them had without the right audio equipment. She was glad the conversation had moved away from personal details.

An hour or so later, Linda replaced the cap on the wine bottle and handed it to Russell. 'I'm off now; Grandpa likes an early night these days. See you tomorrow.'

She drove home carefully, aware of the two glasses of wine she had drunk. Her grandfather had swapped his car for hers, saying her need for reliable transport was the greater, and she appreciated the smooth and silent ride of the Mitsubishi hybrid. Her Ford Focus was fine for him, he had said, for the little amount of driving he did. She agreed with Russell, she was more fortunate than most, but she felt awkward having him point it out. He had never shown quite so much interest in her family before; their relationship had always centred around work.

She pulled into the drive, then waited for the garage doors to open, and parked. Grandpa was still up but had switched off the television and after greeting her, saying Maisie had been fine, he said goodnight. Linda checked on her daughter just to be sure and also just for the pleasure of seeing her face flushed with sleep.

She found herself thinking about Russell again. He had been different from usual. She had sensed some aggression around his questions: he might almost have said, 'it's all right for some,' and she had never before thought of herself being better off financially than he was, mainly because she didn't consider that she was. Her grandfather was, yes, and so were her parents, and she had benefitted from that. But her job at the magazine was through her own merit and she paid her way in her grandfather's house. Was he being snobbish? She couldn't work it out. Perhaps he had some debts, but it would be pointless resenting her for that. She put him out of her mind after deciding she would think twice the next time he suggested they meet for a drink. Coffee at lunch time might be more suited to their relationship.

Chapter Two

Two uneventful weeks passed when she thought little more of Russell. Their conversations were casual and brief at work. Russell complained about his younger brother, his girlfriend and his job and she had murmured sympathetically, but deadlines for work kept her busy and at home, Maisie was suffering with a stuffy nose making her fractious at night. Linda was tired and was once again reminded of the fact that her grandfather was too old to cope with disturbed nights. She found it difficult enough waking up several times in the night, what must it be like for him? He denied it was a problem, telling her that older people did not need so much sleep, and she had to admit there was some truth in this since he spent fewer hours sleeping than she did. She had put Maisie to bed early, after putting some vapour rub on her pillow and now she settled back to catch up on her emails.

One of them stood out: the beginning of the message in the 'subject' box was half visible. *'How is Maisie? Is she feeling...?'* She didn't recognise the sender and it was a 'no reply' address. Should she open it? It must be someone from the nursery school, who knew Maisie had felt unwell, so she thought there was no reason not to. The message continued *'... better? I know how much she means to you.'*

It was signed 'Patsy.' She did not know anyone called Patsy. She dismissed it, but something niggled in her mind. Who at the nursery would feel the need to say, 'I know how much she means to you?'

138

Surely, that was always a given with your child. She finished checking and replying to various friends or domestic updates on bills and decided she would spend the next half hour or so going through Maisie's clothes, quite a few of which needed to be either thrown out or passed on. She went to bed after that and as a way to get to sleep, she thought of all the names of the nursery school staff that she could remember. Patsy still didn't figure amongst them.

The next day, Maisie was much better and Linda said that she would take Maisie to school. Her grandfather didn't argue when she said it would only make her a few minutes late for work. When she got to the school, most of the children, all under five, were either hurtling around the play area on toddler bikes or sorting through a dressing-up box. She left Maisie to decide what she wanted to do and walked over to Sarah who was in charge and asked if there was a 'Patsy' on the payroll.

'No, I don't think so. Ruth will be here in few minutes and Jane is over there. The lady who comes to do the refreshments is called Susan. She may have a stand-in I suppose, on the days I'm not here. You know all the other girls though, don't you? I don't think there is anyone called Patsy. Hang on, I'll ask Jane.'

Sarah returned in a few minutes shaking her head. 'No. No Patsy here. Is there a problem?'

'Not really,' she said, and then explained about the email she had received.

'Perhaps it was one of the mums. I don't know all their first names. I shouldn't worry about it.'

Linda agreed and left, giving Maisie a wave, and receiving a butterfly kiss in return. She then spent an uneventful day working through her lunch break in order to pick up Maisie after school; she planned to resume work from home. She joined the group of parents at the school door waiting for the teachers to identify them before passing over each child. Today, Maisie was holding the hand of another little girl. She was smaller and probably younger than Maisie and had a bright head of copper curls and blue eyes like saucers. Both girls waved at the same time and Maisie looked

139

behind her to see a man with a similar head of curls. The two girls were now jumping up and down with excitement.

'Can April come and play with me?' April was by then bouncing on her father's arm. 'Please, pretty please. May I?'

The man turned to Linda, hand outstretched. 'Hi, I'm Ben. OK with me but that rather depends on where you live?'

'Linda. Nice to meet you! I'm not far, a short walk from here. How about you?'

'We're a five-minute drive, up on Elmstead Avenue. Are you sure it's OK? I could drive you to your place, so I know where my daughter is going to be, if that's all right with you?'

'Absolutely.'

They all piled into the Honda and Linda, feeling rather self-conscious of a sudden, sat silently in the front, ready to point out her grandfather's house. When they drew up outside, Linda turned to him.

'Are you sure this is OK with your wife? I only have to worry about my grandfather – I live in his house.'

'And I only have to worry about my son. He's at primary school and I have to get there in fifteen minutes to pick him up.' He grinned. 'I'll see you later, and thanks.'

'Come back in a couple of hours then,' she said to the closed door: his abrupt departure made her squirm inwardly at the unsubtle way she had asked if he was single.

Grandpa was in the kitchen ready with cold drinks and pieces of apple. The children scooted off to the bedroom to play as soon as they had finished eating and Linda sat at her computer, re-writing and adding to her piece for the magazine. When Grandpa stuck his head round the door a little later, he was grinning. 'Seems like a nice chap.'

'Were you curtain twitching?'

'Just checking. The girls are busy playing with Lego. What's his name?'

'Ben. He's coming back around five. I didn't get involved with a meal for April.'

'Good looking too.'

'I know, and probably single too, but don't hold out your hopes, I think he spends quite a lot of time fighting off the women!'

After finishing her article, she went to join Grandpa in the kitchen. She passed the children who were now playing a game of shops, both adopting very strange voices according to the customer they were pretending to be. There were squeals of laughter as the voices were becoming more and more ridiculous. While they were playing in the other room, Linda made coffee for herself and Grandpa and sat down for a short break before Ben was due to arrive. If it had been a woman coming to collect her child, Linda knew she would have waited and offered her a cup. It was only her sense that Ben would have said no that put her off. It felt too much like she was flirting and it bothered her a bit.

Just then, Ben's car stopped outside.

'There's a boy in the back of the car,' Grandpa said, who was at the window again.

'He did mention he had a son as well;' Linda grinned, 'too much baggage wouldn't you say?'

'In my view, baggage is generally psychological not physical.'

'Wise words. I'd better let him in; he won't be stopping if the boy is in the car.'

Ben looked up as Linda opened the door.

'The girls are in there,' she pointed to the dining room, where the 'shop' was set up.

'Come on, April, Mark's in the car.'

April attempted to interest Ben in their game, but his impatience was hard for them all to ignore. They were gone in a rush of goodbyes and promises to do it again. Linda was glad she had not set her heart on a cosy 'getting to know you chat' with Ben. She reminded herself that she did not have the time any more than Ben evidently did. Also, relationships had not featured in her life in the four years since Paul. She wasn't sure she wanted that to change.

Her article was now finished so she checked her emails before getting a meal for them all. One from her mother, full of news of their latest concerts and possible dates to visit, unless Linda could follow them to an open-air performance next week? She told Grandpa about it, but he was unwilling to commit, saying it was all such a palaver, getting your seats and picnic set up and then freezing to death while the players were all nicely protected under their canopy or whatever. She thought about trying to control a three-year-old in those circumstances and decided he was probably right. Her spirit of adventure had definitely got up and left when Paul did. She sighed and looked at the next message.

'It's nice that...' Once again, an unfinished message was in the subject box. She opened the email. Patsy again! Who was this woman? *'It's nice that you have friends and family who support you. That's good. Patsy.'*

It wasn't anything she should worry about, was it? Except she didn't know who Patsy was, but Patsy seemed to know too much about her. And the 'no reply' address: why was she trying to conceal her identity? Once again, she dismissed it.

Then a few days later she received another one and the message had a different tone. *'Your daughter will be in danger if you don't look after her very carefully.'*

This time it was not a 'no reply' address, and nor was it signed, but Linda guessed it must be Patsy again. Almost without stopping to think, she rattled off a response, her hands shaking. She was angry but now a thread of fear was knotting her stomach.

'I don't know who you are, and I don't want to know. Please stop sending these messages.'

Almost at once, a reply came back.

'How selfish and typical of you. You should think about people less well-off than you and your family.'

Linda re-allocated it into SPAM with a sharp jab of her finger. When the option popped up to report it, she did so, harrumphing loudly

'Everything all right?' Her grandfather looked up, concern on his face.

'Just some rubbish in an email. I don't even know who it was, but they seem to know me.' It was that last bit that agitated in her brain like a worm.

Linda busied herself with the meal and tried to put it out of her mind. It wasn't easy and it disturbed her that someone could be so unpleasant and yet remain anonymous. She didn't know anyone who could be that hateful. After they had eaten, she gave Maisie a bath and put her to bed with a story. She and Grandpa settled down to watch a favourite David Attenborough programme and when that finished, he went off to read a book. Linda switched channels but couldn't find anything to lighten her mood.

The landline rang and she picked it up on the fourth ring. The caller rang off, leaving her saying, 'Hello? Hello? to a void. It did not improve her general feeling of discomfort. Could it have been the same person? If so, why? If it didn't in some way concern Maisie, she would have dismissed the whole thing, but whoever Patsy was, she was right about one thing: Maisie meant everything to her.

At work the next day she asked Russell if he knew anyone called Patsy who might work in one of the other offices. Linda knew *almost* everyone: it was a large open plan area with a few smaller offices for the heads of departments; they were an umbrella company for other magazines as well, but she did not know everyone. Russell had worked there for longer than she had, but his reply was an offhand, 'no.' She was glad she didn't have to explain and she knew she would have prevaricated had he asked.

She settled to work on her next article; this was to be about a group of friends who had set up a business making pot covers, food cages, bread roll pockets and many other things all from colourful ends-of-line cotton material. The group took it in turns to sell them on market stalls across the county and were always looking for new outlets and craft fairs. Talent did not just have to centre around the entertainment business, and Linda was determined to showcase this. Having visited their stall, she was impressed by some of the other craft stalls and wanted to broaden the horizons of the magazine by including them. People wanted to read about success stories which might plausibly be within their own reach and not just the dream world of the overnight pop star. All she had to do was to sell the idea to her boss, Jane.

Predictably, Jane wasn't keen but said she could give it a try as long as she made it interesting and continued with her other work. Linda was enthusiastic and pointed out that most of the gigs they went to were copycats or specialised in underground music which was not to everyone's taste.

A few days later, Linda was ready to hand in the piece she had written, hoping that the photographs she had requested would add interest to the success of the article. She had to work twice as hard that month, preparing two pieces, and was anxious to hear Jane's verdict. She was quite sure that she would reject the whole thing and not allow her to pursue it any further. She had confided in Russell and Dan the photographer, and they had also been less than enthusiastic. Jane had a reputation for brutal honesty, with an emphasis on 'brutal.'

Linda, already feeling dejected by the lack of support, could only hope that Jane would accept it. She was mentally starting on the next month's project and where she intended to find it, but without the go ahead from Jane, she would still have to produce two items. Her mind was still absorbed with plans when her mobile rang.

She took a quick look but did not recognise the number so she dismissed it as not worth picking up. She spent the evening browsing the internet and the local papers for possible sources for her next articles, keeping her eyes open for market venues as well as talent outlets. She wished Jane would be a little more encouraging, after all she could continue doing two pieces, especially if Russell came on board.

Later the next morning, Linda tried to keep busy whilst waiting to hear Jane's decision. By the time she buzzed for her to come in, Linda was a bag of nerves. She sighed with relief when Jane agreed to include the new piece. Jane would never just say 'yes' without her own input and said she wanted to see a more practical approach

144

to the crafts: more depth and explanation and not just about the success or failure as a business venture. Linda felt like cheering. This was a really positive endorsement and she went straight off to tell Russell, who she assumed would come in with her. His reply was scathing.

'If you want to go around those places, fine, but it's a bit too feminine for my liking. I'll stick to the pubs and clubs if you don't mind. In fact, we can split and you can stick to your Women's Institutes and I'll handle the rest on my own.'

Linda glared at him. 'Very fair-minded, I'm sure! I think Jane assumed we would cover them both, together. What's got into you?'

'I want a rise. I'm not sure this is going to help.' He waved a dismissive hand at the piece she had written.

'If we do a good job, and we are doing two pieces instead of one, you could be wrong, surely!'

Russell grunted and informed her he was going to lunch. Linda looked at her watch, 12.30; she felt she could do with a break herself but did not suggest they went together, not if he was going to be moody. She would go and look round the shops on her own instead. He had taken the pleasure out of what she felt should have been a cause for congratulations. He was certainly very grumpy these days, so she tried not to feel depressed at his lack of enthusiasm. Surely it couldn't be him writing those horrible emails, could it?

Linda wandered along the high street, enjoying the brief respite. She had not realised how wound up she had been feeling, waiting for Jane's decision. She had been working extra hard to get both projects finished which had almost put the horrible emails out of her mind for a time, but she knew that the tone of the last one had added to her stress. She took a deep breath and set herself to thinking up new ideas for the next article. She glanced across the road as she passed the coffee house where Russell had probably gone and stopped in surprise. He was with there, and he was with someone, and his companion looked very much like Paul, her ex.

145

She stepped to one side to see more clearly and was convinced she was right. How an earth did they know each other? She did not want to see Paul, or for him to see her. She forgot all about window shopping and turned swiftly back the way she had come, her heart hammering in her chest. She had not seen or heard anything from him since their break-up; he had made his decision completely clear and, as he lived twenty miles away, she had not expected ever to bump into him. Now she felt a surge of anger and hurt as painful as when his rejection had just happened.

She tried to think of what Paul and Russell might have in common, or if he was aware that she even knew him. Nothing came to mind, although she recalled that Paul knew where she worked. After Maisie was born, she had sent him details of her new address at her grandfather's house and also her work and home numbers. She felt it was the right thing to do but made it clear that she did not want anything from him. Even so, a small part of her hoped he might show an interest in his daughter now that she was a little person with a name and not just a detail that could be dismissed so coldly. At the time, she had been hurt by his lack of response and had resolved that would be her last attempt at involving him. She also knew for sure she would never go back with him.

When Russell returned a little later, he was in a strange mood, avoiding looking at her and unusually quiet. She was tempted to ask him what his connection to Paul was, but in the end, she decided she did not want to know. Just the thought of it made her feel tired: that chapter of her life was closed and any stirring of interest that she felt should be utterly quashed or it would be a denial of her decision to forget him. More than a little distracted, she did her best to concentrate on her work.

It was several days later when she received another email. Apparently, the junk filter was not very effective and her heart lurched uncomfortably when she read another unfinished sentence in the subject line: *'How much do you care about...'* She had to read on, she couldn't help herself. *'...about Maisie? In terms of hard cash?'* It wasn't signed again and she realised with a jolt that the

146

sender's address was different again. That's how it had got through her junk filter. But she knew without a doubt this was the same person. Her emotions were a tumult of anger and fear. She decided a phone call to the police was now essential.

The call took forever as she tried to explain to a switchboard for the regional police just what the problem was. After telling her how seriously they took these sort of threats, they put her on to a woman police constable who ended up telling her there was nothing they could do about it. There was not enough to go on, and in their eyes, it was not a serious enough threat. She was advised to continue sending it into her junk file and to try to put it behind her. She tried to argue her case but they insisted that no physical violence was threatened and nor did it constitute blackmail. What about the psychological threat, the understated intimidation which every line screamed out to her? she asked, but it made no difference. They were very understanding, but adamant that the email address was impossible to trace to anyone. Internet bullying was part of life these days. Perhaps she could ask herself who might be capable of such malice? Whoever it was knew enough about her for this to include her email address. Her contact list, she replied, had hundreds of addresses, quite a few of them she could no longer remember why she had them or who they were.

'There's your starting point then,' the WPC said, 'change your email address and only give your new address to the contacts that you trust.'

The WPC seemed very pleased that she had solved her 'little problem,' and quickly ended the call. Linda agreed that it was actually a very good starting point and immediately set to work. It took ages. She could not believe how many there were. They included suppliers of items she had bought in the past and who had insisted on a contact for newsletters and updates, despite never buying from them again. She was ruthless in her deleting process and felt satisfied with the result. She then set up a new email address and sent it to her new slimmed down list of contacts. She went to bed that night satisfied that she had at last done something

147

positive to prevent it happening again. It somehow put the whole thing into a better perspective for her. It wasn't until sometime later that she awoke in the night feeling uneasy, as if there were ghosts lurking in every shadow of the room.

She got up and drank a glass of water when her mind suddenly cleared with a thought that hit her like a physical blow. 'Patsy,' or whoever it was, knew more than just her email. She shuddered with the implications of this. 'Patsy' knew that she had 'friends and family,' and that her daughter was called Maisie and had felt unwell, and she also knew that her family were not poor. These thoughts slammed into her and she put the glass down with a hand that shook. She went to look at her sleeping daughter, who lay peacefully cuddling her favourite floppy eared rabbit.

Maisie was safe. She went back to her room and sat on the bed and tried to think rationally. Surely, these were things anyone could divine. She went through them one by one. People only had to look at her grandfather's house to know they weren't poor. Also, it was safe to assume that most people had friends and family who cared for them. And there were quite a few people who knew her daughter's name and that she had been unwell a few weeks ago, but that didn't mean they knew where she lived did it? The policewoman had said that no threats had been made and she was right. The threats were subliminal and unstated. It was a fear, the sender was telling her, which could be appeased with cash. How much cash? And how did she know it would end? Having told the WPC and not received any sort of comfort, not even the satisfaction of unburdening a problem because they were incapable of solving it, she now felt utterly alone.

The next day was Saturday and Linda planned a trip to the recreation ground where there were swings and slides. There were usually several children who Maisie chatted to and she looked forward to them both being able to enjoy the last days of summer. Once there, Linda pushed Maisie on the swing until her arms and back ached and then sat down on a wooden seat, dedicated to a long-deceased grandmother, and took out her phone whilst still keeping an eye on her daughter as she queued for her turn on the slide. No one was pushing or shoving so she felt confident that Maisie was all right. She glanced around, looking for a face she might know, but there were just a few parents who were busy chatting and caring for their children. She was surrounded by laughter, sunshine and normality.

She pulled up the email and replied: *'What do you want?'* and pressed 'send.' She felt sick.

Chapter Three

The emailer was getting anxious and that was making him angry. The emails he had sent had not been having the desired effect. Linda, that complacent middle-class cow, was not rushing to appease him with offers of cash to stop harassing her as he had expected. He didn't know what tactic to employ next. He didn't intend giving up, although it had crossed his mind. Then he almost cheered when the response came up that he'd been waiting for. At last, she was taking the initiative. She was asking, *'what do you want.'*

'£5k' he swiftly replied. But somehow it didn't make him feel as good as it should. Was it enough? He should have asked for £10k, she could afford it. Why hadn't she asked more questions, begged him to leave her alone, before jumping straight in? He waited to see what her response would be. But nothing happened because Linda was busy. He was nervous, being the one to have to wait. She should have come back at once, asking for the how and the where, or begging him to lay off. He felt as if the balance of power had shifted.

When Linda returned from the recreation park, she saw that an ambulance was parked in the road outside the house. She ran up to the front door, which was closed as she would have expected. Perhaps the ambulance was for someone else, and she found herself saying over and over again under her breath, 'I hope it's not Grandpa, I hope it's not Grandpa.'

Maisie tugged at her hand. 'What's the matter Mummy, why are we running? Is it tea-time? Are we late for tea?'

'No, darling, we're not late; I think we may have visitors though.' She quickly unlocked the door and found a medic standing on the other side. 'What's happened?' She looked around wildly to see where her grandfather was.

'It's all right love; are you the granddaughter? Linda, is it?'

'Yes, yes I am. Where's my grandfather?'

'He's comfortable at the moment. He had a bit of a turn but luckily, he was able to call us. He's having a lie down on the sofa; come and see.'

She followed the young woman into the room where another medic had hooked her grandfather up to all sorts of bits of technology to take his blood pressure and temperature and heaven only knew what else. He had his eyes closed and looked tired and grey, and her heart flipped at the sight of him. She looked down at her daughter whose eyes were round with shock and she suddenly realised how frightening this must be to her. She looked at the medic, hoping she would understand. She did. Linda held her daughter's hand out to the other woman: 'Show the lady where we keep the biscuits, Maisie and have a little treat.' She trotted obediently away and Linda turned her attention back to her grandfather.

'What happened? How is he?'

Her grandfather's eyelids fluttered and he managed a weak smile. 'I'm still here, you know.'

'Yes, you are, Mr Crowther, but it's time we got you into the hospital where they can run some more tests. Now that your granddaughter's here we can get you on your way.'

'Can I go with you?' Linda asked.

'There won't be much you can do except sit in a waiting room, not much fun for your little girl. Why don't you leave him with us

150

for a bit, then you can ring us in a couple of hours, maybe give yourself time to get a babysitter?'

She had to agree, a hospital was no place for a three-and-a-half-year-old. She watched the two medics suddenly speed up as they packed away their instruments, and efficiently placed her grandfather on a gurney. It all happened so fast she barely had time to kiss him goodbye and wish him well. She felt dazed and unable to think about feeding herself or Maisie. The roast dinner she had prepared earlier just needed to be popped in the oven but it looked very unappetising now; she wasn't hungry anymore.

'Shall we have pasta and bacon, Mummy? You know you like that.' She hugged Maisie for being so grown-up. Food was important to Maisie.

'You can help me then. You can cut up the bacon with your scissors while I put the kettle on for the pasta. Then we can make a lovely sauce with some cheese in it.'

Linda put the radio on and they worked together listening to music. It was calming and a long way from how she was actually feeling. No one had mentioned 'strokes' or 'heart attacks.' The medics hadn't said he had fallen over, and she realised she had no idea what had happened to her grandfather nor where it might lead. She ought to ring her father: Grandpa was his dad. The open-air concert was in the next county, not too far away and she was sure both her parents would want to see him. Then she would call her sister, who she hoped might look after Maisie for her.

Linda phoned her father's mobile as soon as they had eaten. He was shocked and full of guilt that it had been so long since he had seen his father and said he would phone later when he had had the chance to speak to her mother and make arrangements to come back. The concert would finish the next evening. He couldn't miss it and he wanted reassurance from her that this would all right, but she couldn't give it. After speaking to the hospital, she would know more, she told him. Then she phoned her sister, Selma. This was even more difficult. Her sister was full of criticisms as to why she had not noticed he was ill, which no matter what she said, Selma was sure there would have been indications she had missed. If not, then Linda must have been expecting too much from him. It made it even harder for Linda to ask her to look after Maisie but in the end, she had no choice. She found herself agreeing that it was all her fault, which made her feel worse. When she had finally calmed down, Selma said she would come over later, leave her own children at home with a neighbour and they could both go to the hospital and take it in turns to look after Maisie outside in the gardens. Linda agreed but said she would phone the hospital first to get an update.

The hospital receptionist was very kind, and she didn't have to wait long to find out what was happening. Her grandfather had suffered a heart attack and was being prepared for bypass surgery. More would be known when he came out of the theatre, but he would not be able to see anyone until tomorrow. She would phone back in a couple of hours as they suggested, to check he was all right after the operation. Maisie could watch some TV, giving them both the time they needed to calm down before the soothing ritual of bath and story and bed while trying to stay focused on the present. She waited until her daughter was soundly asleep before again picking up the phone to call the hospital.

The waiting seemed endless before the receptionist had tracked down the latest developments regarding her grandfather. Once again, she was told he was comfortable, which sounded like a mantra they said to everyone. They were unwilling to commit to anything more positive and emphasised the seriousness of the operation. They said she could definitely visit him tomorrow. She dreaded having to relate all this again to her family, but did so straight away, planning to meet up with Selma the next day. At least, Linda thought with relief, she would be able to put off seeing her sister for another twenty-four hours.

It was getting late by the time she finished with phone calls and she felt emotionally drained. She poured herself a large glass of wine and sat with her feet up and her eyes closed and at last, the worrying thoughts of her grandfather's illness and what it was going to mean to the three of them gradually seeped into her mind. Maisie would miss his solid presence in her life if he did not make a good recovery and she herself would feel the loss of his cheerful and dependable company. Also, on a practical level, she would need to find someone who could take care of Maisie after nursery school and in the holidays, of which there seemed to be so many. Her mind was a cruel ally, jumping ahead of her heart like this. And Russell was right, she had been very lucky, until now.

Perhaps it was that thought which spurred her to check her emails, and it brought her up with a jolt. She quickly scanned through them and there it was.

'Did you not get it? I said £5k and if you continue to ignore me it goes up. I know where you live. Leave the money in a Tesco's shopping bag in the bin by the trolleys near the entrance in Tesco's car park.'

She was furious. Who did this person think she was, able to draw out cash with no explanation to the bank and leave it so that anyone could pick it up in such a public space? The whole thing suddenly seemed ludicrous and she laughed out loud. Who was this idiot? The last few hours had shifted her perspective. Worry and concern for everyone had made her see things differently. This person must be someone very young or at least, not very mature. Someone, perhaps, like Russell's annoying brother. She smiled, but it was more of a grimace. She emailed him back, suddenly convinced she was right.

'When?' she wrote. When he replied saying *'12.30 tomorrow,'* she was certain.

Chapter Four

First thing the next morning, Linda took Maisie to her nursery school early. Lots of parents took their children from 8am onwards, but Linda had only ever done it once before. The school would bill her at the end of term she discovered, and Maisie could even have a breakfast snack as well. Perfect. Having watched her happily playing with a toy tea set, Linda then went to her parent's home to check they had arrived. They had, and she stayed long enough to drink coffee with them and to hear the result of her father's phone call to the hospital. Grandpa was doing well and was 'comfortable' as usual. They would visit at 11am, and Linda would save her own visit to coincide with Selma's, as he wasn't allowed more than two people at his bedside. So far so good.

Now for the difficult part. She drove to the office, first to see Jane and assure her that her pieces were on schedule and then explained she needed a few hours off after lunch to visit her grandfather and pick up her daughter. She would be able to put in a couple of hours but then she would work from home. Jane was sympathetic for a change, knowing that Linda would not let her down. She said Linda could choose her hours, at least for the next few days. Later, with the bones of her article sketched out, she went to find Russell at his desk.

'It's 12.15. Near enough to your lunch break and I need you to come with me, do you mind?'

'OK. What's the problem?'

'Actually, I'd rather not say, just in case I'm wrong. We're going to Tesco's, just up the road.'

He pulled on his jacket, looking worried. 'All very mysterious, hope it's worth it.'

They walked along the road, and Linda pulled him into the doorway of Tesco's as soon as they got there. She then hung a Tesco's bag on the bin outside the entrance. Inside the bag was a cheap paperback novel wrapped in another bag. She hoped it would have the appearance of what she imagined £5000.00 might look like in £50.00 pound notes. She hoped that the annoying brother was as clueless about the size this might be as she was.

She looked at her watch. 12.28. Russell looked at her, one eyebrow raised. She put her finger to her lips as she pulled him into the doorway out of sight. She watched as a youth darted out from

154

behind a car, wearing dark jeans and a hoodie. She heard Russell's sharp intake of breath as he stepped forward. She pulled him back, miming silence.

The lad, undisputedly the annoying brother, snatched up the bag and ran. He slowed after a few strides, long enough to look inside. Unable to see anything except another bag, he ducked behind a car to check the contents more thoroughly.

'If that is your annoying brother, as I believe it is, he thinks I have just given him five grand.'

'What?'

'He's been emailing me, with insults and information he could only have got from you, Russell, and trying to scare me into parting with my well-earned wages so that he won't touch my daughter.'

'Ah no! Really? The little sod! I'll get him for this.'

'That's all very well, and I hope you do punish him, but what the hell have you been saying to him about me? When will you get it into your skull that I am not rich!'

Russell did have the grace to look embarrassed. 'He's mixed up: thinks everyone has more than him. I told you he was a retard.'

'Bit like you then. And while we are having this little chat, how do you know Paul Maynard?'

'Paul? We play squash together.'

'Did you know he's Maisie's father?'

Russell fingered his collar. 'Yes, he told me. Look. I'm going to get hold of Danny before he disappears. We'll talk later, I promise.'

He ran off to where the annoying brother, having unravelled the package from the inner bag, was now gaping at the novel in his hand which should have been a wad of notes. Linda smiled, a genuine grin this time, for the first time in twenty-four hours and went to meet her sister at the hospital.

Grandpa was looking frail but happy. He had been visited by Linda's parents, the first time he had seen them in several months, so that was enough to make him happy. Now that Linda was there with Selma, his day was made. They made a fuss of him: they gave him books and grapes and then he brought them up to date about his treatment. He would be able to come home in a few days, but that brought a frown to his face.

'How is Maisie? How will you cope?'

'You're not to worry. Selma is going to help and we are getting a company to supply someone to come in every morning.'

'I'm not incapable! I'm just thinking about Maisie!'

'I know. But you're going to have to take things a bit easy for a while. Don't worry, I know you'll soon be back on your feet. We just want to take care of you until then.'

The two young women left him with puzzle books and magazines as well as his beloved Inspector Morse books. On the way to the car park, Linda told Selma about the emails and how that had ended up. They had a good laugh, until Selma looked thoughtful.

'D'you know what? It sounds as if you had two different people emailing you. You said yourself that the last addresses were different from the first ones.'

'I suppose that's possible, yes. I've scrubbed them now but I might still be able to find them to show you. We'll have a look later.'

'Sorry, I can't come back with you; I've got to get back: my neighbour won't be able to have the kids for too long. It's not like she has any of her own, they'll be driving her up the wall by now.'

'That's OK. Maisie is staying on at the nursery 'til five.' They parted with a brief kiss and went their separate ways.

When Linda got home, the phone in the house was ringing. Her parents, she thought. They would want to know how Grandpa was. It wasn't though; it was Paul. His voice did not sound the way she remembered it: it was hesitant and lacking the cheerful confidence she associated with him. Immediately she thought of Selma's theory and it made her nervous. Supposing she was right? Her voice was instantly guarded and cool.

'What can I do for you?'

'I want to see you, Lin, no strings, but I sort of want to reconnect. We were good together, weren't we? And lately I've realised you were my best friend and I've never had a better one.'

'Sadly, Paul, you weren't mine though, were you? I could have done with a best friend four years ago, someone supportive, someone kind.'

'I'm sorry, I know and this is difficult, but Linda, I need you.'

'*You* need *me*? And why now?'

'There are reasons, believe me. I'm hoping that maybe we can be there for each other. I know about your grandpa and I'm sorry. He's a lovely guy. How's he doing?'

'He's OK, doing well really but he's eighty-one and it's going to be a slow recovery.'

'Please, Linda, can I come and see you?'

'You haven't even asked about Maisie.'

'I couldn't sort of presume, could I. You know? But of course, I want to see her too.'

'Really?'

'Really. I do. Some things happened in my life. You are the only person I can talk to about it, please Linda, give me a chance.'

'Why should I, all of a sudden, want to be there for you, when you weren't there for me? I needed you, Paul. Half of my child's DNA is yours! Why is everything different just because you need me now? And what could be more important than a child's life?'

'Nothing. Of course not. Nothing. I've grown up since then. The things we used to do together − I've not had that much fun since we split up.'

'Saying that we split up sounds like it was a joint decision. It wasn't. You ditched me.'

'Linda, please. I sent you emails, I'm different now. I want you both in my life.'

'What was that? Those emails scared the hell out of me!'

'That was because Russell's little shit of a brother got hold of the idea of exploiting them. He was eavesdropping when I was talking to Russ outside his house once. Russ just told me what happened;

it's part of the reason I'm phoning: to apologise that it all got twisted.'

'Why weren't you upfront? Why sign yourself 'Patsy'?'

'I thought you'd get that! Don't you remember when we went to a fancy-dress party? I think it was at Kelly's, and I went as Patsy and you went as Eddie, from AbFab.'

'No, I'd forgotten about that.'

'Can I just come and see you, for old time's sake? I'm only in the town.'

'Well, I suppose so.'

'On my way.' He rang off so fast that Linda stood staring at her phone, overwhelmed by a mixture of feelings: annoyance, although he had not been high-handed or overconfident, but also a stirring of excitement. And confusion. That, above all. What did he want?

She had a quick look around and tidied things up. She had not mentioned to Paul that she only had half-an-hour to spare before collecting Maisie from school at five o'clock but she was glad of that. She had an escape route, a way to end their meeting.

He looked different, she thought, when he arrived on the doorstep ten minutes later. She directed him to the kitchen, aware that he was familiar with her parents' home but not this one. He sat at the kitchen table while she poured out the coffee, then sat down opposite and studied him. He lacked the air of confidence he used to exude, but then she must look different to him too, she thought.

'Things have happened, Linda. I went out with other girls, but they weren't you. I missed you.'

'What is it you want, Paul? I've changed. Maisie comes first for me now.'

'Of course. Russ told me your grandfather was helping and now he's ill. Is that going to be a problem for you?'

'I want to take care of him; he's spent the last few years taking care of me, especially when I needed things for the new baby, and then after that, in every other way you can think of. So, what is it, Paul?'

'I want to be there for you – for you and Maisie.'

'I haven't had a relationship since you ditched me and I won't have men flitting in and out of Maisie's life, and that includes you.'

Paul tried not to be put off by her tone, but there was something he needed to tell her. 'I know I can't expect us to pick up where we left off, but I want to get to know Maisie and help. Something happened and it's changed me. I...'

'Not now, Paul. I have had two weeks of stress with Russ's horrible brother, which I hope he will deal with; I've had issues at work which mean I have twice as much to do, and the only good thing to happen this week is that Grandpa is getting better.' She glanced at the clock. 'I have to go now and pick up Maisie.'

'Can I come?'

'No. Maybe another time.'

'I could drop you off, and just see her? Like a passing stranger? I won't even talk.'

She felt she couldn't refuse, then questioned why she should feel that way. It was too complicated and she gave up. 'I suppose it won't do any harm.'

They drove to the school in silence and Linda was determined that Paul would not come back with her. Why should he? she thought. I haven't seen or heard from him in all this time, why should he just walk back into her life like nothing had happened. She glanced at him. Something had happened though, hadn't it? He had wanted to tell her and she had stopped him. 'Not now,' she had said.

Suddenly Maisie was in front of them, still pulling on her coat and already talking about what they might have for dinner. Her gaze glanced over Paul without pause. She stopped long enough to ask, 'How's Grandpops? Did you see him today?'

'He's fine, sweetheart. He's getting better and he'll be home tomorrow. Now say hello to Paul.'

'Hello.' She gave him a shy smile. Paul looked bowled over and Linda couldn't stop the swell of pride and love she felt for her daughter. 'Right. Off we go then. 'Bye Paul.'

Paul looked dazed but she didn't want their conversation to continue in front of Maisie. Too much was going on in their lives right now. She waved and started to walk back home.

I'll ring you then,' said Paul.

'OK.'

Chapter Five

When Linda told Paul she was pregnant, he thought she must be joking. They had such a good life together and he didn't want it to change. Like Linda, he lived at home with his parents, but because hers were always away he spent most of his time at her place. They both had well paid jobs, Paul was a professional photographer, mostly for catalogues but he also did other freelance work to get more money. It was through their combined jobs that they met.

Life was lots of fun: holidays skiing, weekends away doing scuba-diving, visiting places of interest, all sorts of things. Paul thought she loved their life as much as he did and he felt betrayed, let down, when she said she was pregnant. It felt as if she had plotted his downfall. When they split up, he substituted Linda for his mates, trying to get groups together to go off on weekends away, and sometimes he would find a girl who was happy enough to go with him, but they always turned out to want commitment. He started to realise that he had actually had a kind of commitment with Linda, and no one else quite measured up. She had never pushed for a future together, but in his more self-centred moods he wondered if that was why she had got pregnant. Then he would remember that she had been sick and maybe the pill not working was as much a shock to her as it was to him.

Lately, he spent a lot of time feeling angry. His pleasure in life had diminished after they parted and had had turned out not to be the freedom for more excitement he had imagined. He missed her,

160

but he also knew that their life together could never have been the same with a kid in tow.

Then a terrible thing had happened. It was a few weeks ago; he had been driving back from shopping (he had his own place now, no longer living with his parents) when he had swerved to avoid a pigeon in the road. Out of nowhere, a little child was suddenly on his nearside wing. He wasn't going fast but the bang, well, he could still hear that sound in his nightmares. He froze. The mother screamed and ran to her child as he finally recovered his wits and got out of the car. He thought she was dead, though there was not a mark on her. She looked so sweet, with her long blonde hair; but she was not moving. Then she came to, started crying and it was pandemonium. People running to help, a police car stopping the traffic, an ambulance with its siren blaring through the quiet − Paul was in a daze. He kept repeating through shocked tears, 'I thought she was dead.' And all he could think of was that Maisie, the daughter he had rejected and had never seen, must have been about the same age.

He wasn't blamed. So many witnesses said the little girl just ran into the road to see the pigeon, and that he had swerved away from the bird, not into the child. Her mother said she had suffered a hearing loss since birth and the hardest thing had always been calling to her: to stop her from getting into danger. Paul went to see her and her parent's a few days later. She had her arm in a sling from the shoulder injury, but she seemed none the worse. Such a sweet bright child, and the thought stayed with him, haunted him, that it could have been Maisie.

He began to see parenthood in a different light after that. He met Russell, knowing he worked with Linda and asked him where Maisie went to school and what time she finished, so that he could see her, and experience something of what that other parent had felt. He wanted to see Linda as well, and when he did, witnessing their meeting outside the school, it almost made him cry. All that transparent love, it made him realise how much he had lost, how selfish he had been to expect Linda to give all that up for him.

Paul tried to put all of that into words when he met Linda in a local coffee house. He stammered through most of it, hoping that she would see his point of view when he had never tried to see hers.

'Just to see her sometimes, get to know her, take her out, you know.'

Linda looked at him, calculation in her eyes as she shook her head.

'It's not going to happen, Paul. You have missed all the hardest parts: and I have had to cope without your support. Maisie is a lovely child and I am never going to let you swan into her life, give her treats and then disappear. You'll meet someone and then, she will no longer be important.'

'It won't be like that, I promise. I want to be in both your lives.'

'I wanted that too, four years ago. I understand you have had this trauma and it's made you see things differently. Really, I understand. But Maisie is my life now, and I am not going to allow you to have all the best bits, taking her out for treats. Those are *our* treats. There isn't time in my life or hers to have double treats, and by that, I don't mean Disneyland or learning to ski in Switzerland, it's all a lot more low key. It's a trip to the swimming pool or a sleep over with a friend.'

'Of course. Look. Couldn't I just be around for a bit? Come and make supper for you both? Watch TV with her? Play Scrabble?'

'I'll think about it. That sounds okay; I suppose, but you do see my point? I don't see why you should suddenly become a favourite uncle. Fatherhood is a bit more than that.'

Paul leaned across the table and took her hands in his. 'I mean it Linda. I want it to be more than that too. I want to share some of the responsibility. I want to feel like that mother felt about her child when she thought she had nearly lost her. I was so lucky, it wasn't my fault, but it felt like it was. Her love, her fear of loss and her ongoing concern, it felt like a sword in my side, a physical pain. I can't describe the anguish I felt any better than that, but I knew that it changed me, made me more alive and more aware than I have

162

ever been before. I swear to you that I will not let either of you down ever again.'

Linda smiled. She could hear the truth in his voice. She would give him a chance to be the father he wanted to be; she couldn't refuse. Maybe the future would hold disappointments and frustrations for all of them, but she had to give him a chance.

GOING HOME   by S.F. Formi

The rain lashed against the carriage windows, great rivulets pouring down the glass, obscuring the view. The wind, not to be outdone, tore at the train door making it rattle and screech. For the girl, the weather was a distraction, and she busied herself shaking out her umbrella and coat then settling into her corner seat. Soon, she began to doze, her face crumpled against the windowpane, one dark strand of hair curling free of her beret.

Waking abruptly, she reached for a handkerchief to mop the tears she had cried in her sleep. She looked up, embarrassed, though of course the compartment was empty apart from herself. But no, there was a man in the opposite corner, his hat pulled down covering most of his face. He too appeared to be slumbering. Kay didn't remember anyone getting in, or even the train stopping. She glanced at him, frowned and then looked away. The train rumbled on.

The warmth of the carriage, the rhythmic sounds, the jolt and sway – soon Kay was wrapped again in sleep. Some part of her though remained intensely aware of the other passenger: at a certain point she felt, or fancied, that he came and sat beside her. Instead of being alarmed by this, she found the closeness soothing and made no protest when the stranger reached for her hand and clasped it between his own. When she opened her eyes, the man was back in his seat. Had she dreamt that he sat beside her? As she stared at him, he lifted his head and removed his hat. She saw the face, strangely smooth and worry-free, but still the crisp white collar with its pinched tie tugged at her memory.

'Oh,' she said and her hand strayed towards him.

'Don't fret my dear,' he said, 'all will be well.'

The train was juddering to a halt.

'Go now. You must go,' the man spoke again. 'All will be well.'

Kay hesitated, unable to drag her eyes away, then bundled her things together and made for the door. Turning, she saw that he was saying something but it was drowned out by the scream of the brakes and an explosion of steam from the engine. She saw his hand raised in salute and then the carriage door was wrenched open from outside and she almost fell onto the platform.

A young man was running towards her, his face twisted and his mouth working.

'I'm sorry Kay. So sorry. You're too late. Dad's gone.'

Kay put her arms around him. 'I know,' she said, 'I know.'

THE LANGUAGE OF DOORS   by P.C.R. Penfold

The enormous castle gates, once proud and golden in the sunlight, have silvered with the centuries and now they are the colour of a burned-out fire, streaked grey and black. Their purpose now ancient history. An army of men on horseback, clad in metal, would have thundered through, hooves sparking on stone, swords clattering against armour. Women, crowding these stone walls would not have heard the response to their cries of goodbye above the tumultuous noise.

Just as my husband would not have heard my gurgled response to his, 'see you later,' on that terrible morning: my mouth full of toothpaste. Now, these few tranquil moments have abandoned me. Instead, wisps of random conversation drift through my mind. I have just left the crematorium; heavy doors clanged shut to give privacy to the mourners before the next appointed cremation. The sound had been more final to me than his disappearing coffin. None of the people in the chapel of rest had been invited and I could not meet the eyes of anyone there. There would be no wake. My shame was too great.

My thoughts are bitter. Those women from the past who had gathered here, would have known their men might not return. I had not. Our front door, mine now, is dove grey with brass furniture. It had clunked shut, impossible to slam and show anger or finality. It was chosen to look pleasing, welcoming. Hours later, I opened it to the police, a man and a woman in uniform, who waited for my answers to their enquiries. The woman looked sympathetic, the man – just efficient. Identities over, and the worst news delivered, an exchange of information followed:

'What was your husband doing in Cheltenham?'

166

'I don't know, he should have been at work in Stroud.'

'Is this his car?' They showed me a photo, the number plate clearly visible.

'Yes, but he works in a shop! Classic Menswear. He would not have been in his car at 10am.'

Then, the policewoman, her voice suitably grave: 'He wasn't alone.'

'Oh God, was he with another woman?'

'He was with a man.' The policeman rushed on to explain, forestalling another inappropriate question. 'He was driving very fast, to get away from us.'

'But why would he...?'

'He turned a corner, much too fast, straight into a wall. The other man survived, the one holding a bag full of stolen jewellery.'

'But... '

'Can I get you another cup of tea, Beryl?'

No, no, no. I put my face in my hands, rocking back and forth with the pain of memory. The ghosts of women whose husbands had gone to war crowd around me, in front of these towering doors, enveloping me in a grey shawl of grief.

Never to see him again...

But their loss was not like mine, their men had gone to an honourable death, or so some would say.

Never to be able to ask him for the truth...

Never to have really known him at all.

FOLLOWING THE FLOCK   by S.F. Formi

Here we go again. Why we do this I don't know. Flap, flap, flap. How many more miles to go? Him next door reckons it's still over a thousand. What's the point! If only I'd had a proper parent, they might have been able to tell me why we do this. Every year it's the same; no sooner have I settled down and got myself cosy somewhere than some clever twerp tweets that it's time to be off.

So, we're on our way to the UK. The UK, I ask you? It's full of people walking around in masks, afraid of getting near one another. But, and this is not a good thing, they are getting closer to 'nature'. That's great news, isn't it? I don't think! So not only do I have to put up with the usual crazy band of twitchers, now there will be a whole load of amateurs banging about the woods, trying to 'spot' wildlife. That's the last thing I need – bungling idiots peering at me through the branches they've just trampled, at the very moment that I'm looking for that perfect nest. Nobody realises just how hard we have to work to find that special place. House-hunting is quite a chore. These days there's a terrible shortage of suitable accommodation. Not that it's for me of course, but I must make sure it's right for the next generation.

So where are we now? Oh, I see we're just over the Mediterranean so no chance of a rest just yet then. My wings are starting to get tired. That's another thing that's not understood, just how much it takes out of you, this long-distance flying. I'll be a shadow of my former self by the time we get there. Still, we'll be into Spain soon and maybe I'll get hold of some of that chicken paella they do there. I don't let the others know as they get a bit sniffy if you go off the old caterpillar diet. But what's wrong with a bit of variety?

So I've been lucky so far, no storms or gales. You'd be surprised how often we get swept off course, even at this time of year. It's so calm at the moment that that young whippersnapper is trying out wheelies, whirling and spinning, showing us his underneath bits. They are all tut-tutting but me, personally, I don't mind. Let him have a bit of fun. It's a tough old life.

I don't say this too often, but actually I do wonder why we do it. This migrating lark I mean. After all, couldn't we find nests just as good back in Africa? And it's a lot warmer there. You never know what weather you'll get in good old Blighty. In fact, you can have the whole lot in one day: storms, sunshine, wind, sometimes snow as well. I ask you! It's not as if I've got to look for the right materials or a nice location to build my nest. That's already done for me, and I'm sure there'd be plenty of obliging birds in Africa who'd be willing to help out and rear my youngster. Not that I couldn't make a proper job of it myself – if I had to, but why bother? And I've got other ways to spend my time. So, leave it to someone else.

Whoops, what's that down there? Looks like the right sort of place to put up for the night. A bit of woodland, and right next to a village with its own cafeteria. That's a bit of luck. Here goes chaps!

TIME AFTER TIME by S.F. Formi

The garden is still, nothing stirs. A low twittering in the trees as the birds begin to roost is the only sound. It is as if the garden, like the children, is exhausted from the day's activities. To the west the sun is sinking; the last of its rays touching the water in the pond, creating golden puddles amongst the bulrushes. Hollyhocks, delphiniums and lupins march in stately rows up to the house. All is calm and orderly.

The sky begins to darken, streaks of violet and red showing between the dark pines protecting the grounds. From amongst the mounds of hydrangeas, ghostly in their whiteness, comes a rustling. A woman steps out of the shadows to stand by the pond, gazing into its depths. A garden trug sits at her feet – the dead and dying rose petals a medley of pinks and creams.

There is the click of heels on paving stones and a man joins the woman.

'I was expecting you earlier,' the woman says, but she smiles and goes to kiss him.

He coughs and turns away. 'Yes, I'm sorry. It was work.'

'Of course,' she says.

'Are the children in bed?'

'Not yet, they're about to have their bath. I think they were hoping...'

'Look I'm sorry, Celia...' his words trail away.

'For what?' she says. 'You're here now. You can do bath time. They will love it.'

'No, no, I can't.' He is shaking his head, a deep troubled frown on his face.

'What do you mean?' she forces a laugh but pulls her cardigan closer round her body.

'Look,' he says again. 'It's just that, I can't do this anymore.'

'Can't do what?' her voice is tight.

'Can't carry on like this.' He is looking at her directly, then rushes on:

'It's over Celia – between us, it's over.'

'But…' her words come slowly at first, 'we're married, Tom. You can't just tell me it's over, just like that.' As she speaks her tone begins to rise.

He shuffles his feet and loosens his tie.

'But you know, you must know, it hasn't been good; hasn't been working,' he stops, '…for ages.'

'No, I don't know. What I do know is that you find every excuse not to spend time with me, with us, with the children.' Anger is coming to the fore. 'What have I done wrong, tell me? Where did I fail, as a wife? As a mother to our children?'

'No, no. Please don't make this hard.'

'Don't make it hard? What did you expect?'

She gets her handkerchief from her cardigan pocket and twists it in her hands. 'If there is something wrong, why did you not say? We…we, can talk about it.'

'No.'

'What?' her face, tanned from a day in the garden, turns slowly grey.

Two small shadows stand by the back door.

'Daddy's home,' says the little one.

'Yes,' says her sister.

'Are they going to have a kiss and canoodle?' She makes smooching noises with her mouth.

'I don't know. Look at the stars, Titch. Aren't they lovely?'

The girls gaze up at the sky. It's like a dark blue coverlet, sprinkled with twinkling lights.

'It's beautiful, Sis. What are they called?'

'I only know a few. Daddy taught me.'

'Will Daddy teach me?'

'Maybe.'

Their attention switches back to the bottom of the garden. A dove coos a goodnight lullaby, and then there is silence until once again a fierce whispering begins:

'You can't mean it. People don't...don't end a marriage, just like that.' She takes a step closer to him. 'We said our vows, Tom.'

'For God's sake woman,' he blusters, 'we are in the 20th century, the war's over and everything has changed.'

He draws a flat silver case from his pocket, extracts a cigarette and places it between his lips as he searches in his other pockets for his lighter.

She watches, mesmerised by his actions.

'I can't believe the things you are saying. I thought we were...'

'Happy?' he interrupts with a sneer. 'Did you really?'

Shocked, she stares at him in silence.

He finds the lighter and she listens to the familiar, click, click, until it flares into flame. He bends close and the sharp profile of the long straight nose, the black hair swept and Brylcreemed back, comes into focus. All so familiar, but suddenly it is the face of a stranger. How had she thought she knew this man, she wonders?

The children see the spark of the cigarette lighter.

'Daddy's having a fag,' says the little one.

'You mustn't use that word,' says her sister.

'Why not? You say it.'

'It's slang, and I'm older than you, so it's different.'

'When I grow up, I'm going to have a long cigarette holder and I'll have a handsome man to light every fag I smoke, as they do in the pictures.' She puts her fingers to her lips as if holding something there, then blows out as if blowing a smoke ring.

Silence.

'Sis, what will you do when you grow up?'

'Oh, I don't know. I'll probably have to get a job.'

'But don't you want to go dancing and have lots of men taking you out in their fast cars?'

'Maybe.'

Splashing and shrieking noises come from upstairs. Childish babble and laughter accompany the sounds.

'It's that new family.'

'Why are they in our house, Sis?'

Sis sighs, 'you know why.'

They hear another sound, an insistent bleep and then a voice calls out.

'Mike, that's my zoom conference, can you shut the kids up please?'

'Bit difficult, Jen. They're in the bath and you know what they're like. Why don't you take it downstairs?'

'Oh, for heaven's sake. This working from home is a nightmare. But don't worry, Mike. If I lose my job we can always live on your salary, can't we?'

'Probably not,' Mike mutters.

'It's funny, isn't it Sis?'

'What is?'

'That lady seems to think she is more important than the Daddy, doesn't she?'

'Does she?''

'Why isn't she looking after the children?

'I don't know Titch. I suppose things change.'

'Is Daddy coming in now do you think?'

'I don't know.'

The girls peer out into the dark garden and the world becomes silent again. It is shattered by a cry.

'Please, please don't...Don't go Tom.'

The children hear the anguish. Titch creeps closer to her sister, who takes her hand, soft and sticky with the residue of tea-time bread and jam. A light breeze sends the sweetness of honeysuckle and roses into their faces as they hear their father's footsteps receding out of the garden.

'Mike,' the voice comes again, 'pour me a drink, will you darling?'

A man comes into the kitchen and the two girls slide outside and into the shadows. He clatters around with glasses and bottles and holds a drink out to the woman who comes down the stairs and joins him.

'Mm, lovely,' she says. 'I needed that.'

'How was the conference call?' he asks as they move onto the decked area outside.

'Do you want the good news or the bad news?' She takes a large swallow from her drink.

'Just tell me.' Mike frowns as he twirls his glass and studies the wine.

'OK,' she takes a deep breath. 'Well, they're talking about redundancies – a lot.'

'Will it affect you?'

'Don't know yet.'

They remain sitting in silence.

It is dark now; a few soft sounds come from the bushes. Jen ducks as a bat flies close. Mike leans back in his chair, breathing in the fragrance of the stocks planted by the door. The night wraps around them like a velvet shawl.

Jen gets up and throws a switch on the wall, light floods the deck and Mike blinks.

'Why did you do that? It was so peaceful.'

'To stop the bats coming too close of course.'

'Of course,' he grimaces. He begins, 'We've got cucumbers coming and the lettuces will be ready to eat very soon.'

She laughs, 'Oh you and that veg patch.'

'Well, you might show some interest. It's been a lot of work.'

'I'm worried, Mike. Don't you understand?' She leans forward, reaching for the bottle on the table between them. 'How will we afford all this if I lose my job?'

174

Mike says nothing but mimics her action and refills his own glass. They are both quiet. From the end of the garden, they hear some sibilant sounds.

'What was that?' she says.

'Maybe a cat?'

'Making that noise?'

Mike gets up to investigate and as he gets closer to the pond, there is movement at the back of the white hydrangea and then he hears a sound. He stands rock still for a moment; there is a strange sensation, the air seems charged with some sort of tension. He turns his head to listen.

As he comes back up towards the house, a movement catches his eye. It is at the side of the deck, just outside the beam of light. It's probably an animal, he thinks.

'What was it?' she says

'Nothing there, but...' he pauses.

'But what?'

'I thought I heard footsteps.'

'Footsteps! Didn't you investigate?'

'There was nothing there I tell you!'

'For God's sake, Mike.' She gets up and stomps off indoors.

Mike sits, nursing his glass. He looks around, trying to peer into the bushes. There is something, he is sure, but what it is he can't tell.

The girls' attention is focused on the couple by the pond.

'Tom, Tom,' she is running after him. Light steps following his heavier ones. Sis sighs, how many more times? she wonders, and pulls Titch further into the shadows until they are invisible.

THE CIRCUS CAME TO TOWN   PCR. Penfold

I suppose I should have guessed what might happen, and then I could have prevented at least part of the outcome of that fateful meeting. But let me start at the beginning.

The circus was in town: a small affair, with performing dogs, a tethered monkey winding an organ, acrobats in strange, colourful outfits and clowns with painted faces. The children loved it and you could see that the adults were enjoying it too.

It was also an excuse for market stalls from far and wide to set up with their home grown produce and handicrafts. I wandered through the streets and was soon approached by a woman selling pots of skin cream. She said it had healing properties and that it had cured her son's eczema. She claimed it cured all sorts of skin ailments and blemishes and was especially beneficial to ageing skin, and for proof she pointed to her own smooth, mahogany face, saying she was sixty years old. She held it out to me with one hand, the other outstretched for money. I guessed she had come with the circus but was now too old to perform and had fallen on hard times.

I was charmed by her; she was exotic and persuasive and I bought a jar despite the equally exotic price, thinking at the time of my own son's allergies and skin problems. Once home, I used it for a variety of things, and every time, the condition: the cut or bruise or sore was improved or cured in a few days. I told everyone about the cream because I had discovered that the woman had stayed in the area, and as I had suspected, had been abandoned by the circus. Friends, neighbours and relatives bought her cream and the woman's sales soared.

She was happy and grateful for this improvement in her circumstances; she had been struggling for many months to make a living. Nevertheless, people were afraid of her. She wasn't like the rest of us, with her mass of frizzy black hair which stuck up around her round, dark face, and although her creams were undoubtedly beneficial, was that entirely normal? The whispers began, and I wasn't the only one who had described her potions as magical.

There were zealots among us who thought her claims were blasphemous and soon, an evil mood overtook the praise and she was labelled 'witch.' This vicious gossip was fed by fear of her, but the bullies and the bigots joined ranks and plotted to get her. One dark and rainy evening, her pockets full of coins from creams all sold, they jumped her.

They would not be appeased by her screams of denial. They put a bag over her head and dragged her to the river where the ancient ducking stall still rested, long unused and no longer legal. She screamed and did her best to free herself, calling repeatedly to have pity for the sake of her son, but she was overcome by their number.

Her shrieks rang out as she was tied to the chair and ducked in the dank and filthy depths, over and over again, and then abandoned, her outline wavering and her mouth gaping. No one stopped them. This I was told, because her screams had raised some interest and an audience of over twenty people had watched her die, but I could not bear to witness it.

I spent days looking for her son, as I had heard he had been left to roam the streets to find food, and a bed where he could shelter from the night's chill. I searched the alleyways asking if he had been seen, feeling some responsibility for his mother's death, and I spent sleepless nights, remorseful that I had somehow caused it by extolling her products so highly. But I gave up too easily when perhaps I should not have. I should have carried on.

I awoke from another restless night to the sound of spluttering and gurgling. I guessed it was my own snoring until I heard it again, now, with my eyes fully open. I felt my skin crawl and my nightclothes which were clinging to my body, were cold and wet. I cried out and my husband came to me. He looked at me with fear in his eyes, for I was sweating and red in the face. He said he would call the doctor as I slipped into an uneasy state of semi-consciousness. My breath rattled in my throat, and I heard that woman's shrieks of fear and the gurgling she undoubtedly made as her breath left her body. I had no doubt that it was she, that elderly black woman.

'It wasn't my fault,' I croaked, 'I meant you no harm. It was just my way. I never called you a witch.'

My ramblings continued, hour on endless hour, and my body felt it was drowning in its own internal fluids. The doctor confirmed pneumonia and said the next few days were crucial to my recovery.

Gradually the images of that woman's face, which was no longer as beautiful as a burnished chestnut but was now an ugly shriven grey, ceased to haunt my waking and sleeping hours. Slowly, my temperature became stable. Steadily, I recovered. But now I had a mission, something to live for. I had heard her voice in my head, seen her silent mouthing, and her message was unmistakable. I should not have given up: I must find that woman's son and care for him as one of my own.

My husband joined in my search, fully supporting my wild story, having seen the effect it might have on my health should he choose to ignore me. We stooped in doorways, searched in derelict buildings, turned over rags and saw many sad and pitiful sights. Weeks went by and I began to have the most terrible dreams. The black woman's face appeared to me, so close to mine I could feel her breath. Her eyes would widen, huge and glaring into mine as she screamed, 'Find him! Find him!' I would awaken, soaked in cold sweat, and so I would set off again to search the streets. I could not abandon the task, though I was neglecting my wifely duties and the care of my own family. So many times, I was exhausted to the point of giving up, and then the dream would return to haunt me.

Finally, we heard tell of a boy whose skin was dark as mahogany and whose hair was a wiry black halo around his head; a child who was thin and half starving who ran from all who approached him and would only eat the food offered to him if it was left on the

178

ground. Then he would advance and snatch it up to his mouth whilst running away as fast and as far as his spindly legs would take him. I knew that he was the one.

We won his confidence with titbits and fruit and waited for him to come back for more, which was always there waiting for him, as were we. We left him clothing as well as food; and finally, we coaxed him into the open, and then, like a stray dog, he would take food from our hands. Then we talked to him, of his mother and his life. We offered him our home and we were honoured and relieved when he accepted.

At last, I felt at peace, and slept calmly at nights. The boy remained with us until he was fully grown, forever grateful for our own outstretched hand. In time, he learned to accept the colour of his skin as different, but that could not be said of everyone else, but he had his mother's stoical nature and it won him many friends.

BIRD PROOF   by P.C.R. Penfold

Jenny awoke that morning, as she had almost from the first day, with murder in her soul. Patience, she muttered to herself. Be patient, think calm thoughts, and even though the squawking, pig-like sounds were still echoing around the garden, she took three deep breaths and closed her eyes. Carl was leaving for work, wobbling on his bicycle around the gate in an effort not to let out the geese, but they followed him, snapping at his heels, then rushing back in as soon as he turned to close it, squawking their arrogant little heads off.

Reluctantly, she got up. Perhaps if she fed the ungrateful geese now, they would allow her to water the flowerpots in relative peace. Before they ate them. She had hoped that feeding them, which of course she would do anyway, might create a bond of friendship between them. So far, no bond existed. She threw them a handful of corn and watched as the two, yes, just two were making that awful row, feasted as if they had not been fed for a week.

Jenny and Carl had moved in a few days ago, and the old couple who owned the cottage before, had moved to a little terrace in the high street, with no garden to speak of. They told her they had a smallholding once and the two geese were all that remained. Neither the RSPB nor the animal rescue centre could accommodate them, the latter saying they didn't have enough space and also, the geese were likely to upset all the other birds in their care. Jenny could believe that; they were pretty frightening when they ran towards you. They would rehome them as soon as possible, they assured her with ironic empathy, which Jenny recognised was completely insincere and meant that they did not consider it a priority.

180

Finishing with the watering, she looked at the garden. She had great plans for it, because at the moment it was a flattened area where the geese roamed unchecked, stamping down the slightest indication of a weed, let alone a flower or a blade of grass. She sighed and left them to it. They were not so much frightening, as disruptive and destructive. Back indoors, she continued unpacking boxes and finding homes for the contents.

The next morning, she awoke to silence and wondered what it was that was missing.

'Can you hear anything?' she said to Carl.

'No? Should I?'

'No, but that's rather the point. I can't hear the geese. Quick, they might be in trouble, a fox or something.'

They both scrambled out of bed, putting on whatever came to hand and tumbled down the stairs to the back door. Then the honking started. The geese were fine, but today they were accompanied by two goslings: fluffy, grey, round, and adorable.

'Did you know they were nesting?'

'I never thought about it. I haven't been watching them all day, I've been unpacking. Does that mean the RSPB won't take them now?' Jenny looked at Carl as if he should know the answer, which of course, he didn't.

'Haven't the faintest.'

'I'll ring them later, they might need some attention, the goslings, that is.'

They turned to go, closely followed by two irate parents, honking their own carefully orchestrated version of 'get back to where you belong.'

Jenny phoned the vet and was assured the geese and their offspring would be fine and could be left alone to get on with it. 'Are they always so cross?' she asked.

'Oh, they're not cross. They're just marvellous guard dogs.'

Jenny wasn't convinced and went back to talking to clients on the phone about their insurance policies and hoped the geese would keep quiet. Her mind was not on the job.

She went outside with a cup of coffee and wandered up to the pond to see if she could find the goose nest. The parents flapped and squawked their welcome and she stared in surprise at what she saw. There were now four goslings, or perhaps there always had been. She sat down and looked at them thoughtfully. Perhaps, if no-one was prepared to help, and it was getting less and less likely as the family grew, she and Carl should consider breeding them? They were beautiful: glossy white feathers, bright mandarin beaks and those eyes, so piercing and knowing.

Later that day, there was a ring at the door, accompanied of course, by squawking geese and closely followed by sharp knuckles rapping staccato fashion on the window. Jenny rushed to open it, summoned by the urgency of it all. A woman stood there, looking flustered, and anxiously pointing at her car.

'I have a duck! Oh! You're not Mrs Fotheringale are you!'

'No, they've moved. Is something wrong?'

'There was this duck, in the road, just *asking* to be run over, so I threw my coat over it. It has obviously got clipped wings and it's not injured or anything. I thought, you know, Mrs Fotheringale...well, I was told she would have taken it in, but if she's nor here...'

'No, as I said, I'm afraid they've moved. Where is it now?'

The woman waved her arm in the direction of the car again. 'In the boot.'

'You can't leave him there can you. We have got a pond, so I suppose...let's go and see him. Err, is it a he?'

'I think so, probably, he's got shiny green bits, and er, looks quite fierce.'

'I'm beginning to think it's their default position, these game birds.'

'Perhaps they know we like eating them!'

182

Jenny picked up the bird and plonked it straight down on the grass, giving the woman back her slightly messy coat, and they both watched as the duck waddled off, heading instinctively for the pond.

'Of course, they might not get on with the geese. I'll have to phone the RSPB again.'

She did so and was reassured. In fact, they said, as the duck had clipped wings, it was safer with the geese. Jenny went back to work, feeling unexpectedly cheerful.

By the end of the week, they had also acquired a peacock, courtesy of the duck woman. Jenny said to Carl how nice it was to be getting to know people so quickly and learning new skills concerning the care of wild fowl; and having a project. They should be thinking about fencing off part of the garden to include the pond, so that Jenny could also have a nice garden that wasn't covered in bird poo.

With the arrival of this new guest, Jenny decided she would contact Mr and Mrs Fotheringale. She rang and received an invitation to come and have tea that afternoon. There were quite a few questions Jenny now felt she could ask about care of the birds and how it was that the Fotheringales had managed to call a halt to this influx, and then disposed of them all except two geese before moving?

Her knock on the front door was timid. She remembered the woman as being frail and the husband as chatty. Once they were settled, Jenny brought them up to date with all the bird news, and then asked how they managed to re-home the birds they had rescued.

'It was the foxes, you know...'

'That's horrible! How many? And even with the geese squawking?'

The couple looked at each other, and later, when Jenny reported this to Carl, she used the word 'guiltily' to describe it. She sipped her tea and decided not to ask why they had never built a cage or fenced off an area to provide sanctuary for the birds. Perhaps they couldn't afford it; after all, they had downsized their home. She left as soon as she could, feeling that something had not been quite right.

Arriving back, she smiled tolerantly at the geese, aware that her feelings had changed towards them since the arrival of the goslings, but they seemed even more agitated than usual and glancing around, she could see why. A sickening sight of feathers and blood which, on closer inspection, she could see was the peacock. Poor, elderly and bedraggled creature that he was, he now lay strewn in bloody bits outside the bike shed. She remembered what the Fotheringales had told her about the fox; he must be a crafty fellow to have attacked in daylight hours and braved the hostile geese, she thought. She let herself in the house and found gloves and a bag to pick up the mess. Holding it with distaste, she noted that the neck had been severed, cleanly, with something sharper than fox teeth. She felt a chill go through her. She noticed something else: the poor bird had arrived with very few of his magnificent feathers, but they were all missing. This was not the work of a fox. Who then? And how did they get past the geese?

Once again, she called the RSPB. They told her that reports of this kind had filtered through from time to time, though none had ever come directly from her address.

'What do you mean?'

'A neighbour once reported that your predecessors were mistreating their dog, which in turn, was savaging the ducks.'

'This is different; someone has been here and killed the peacock.'

'You should report it to the police; an intruder is not something we can deal with. Also, it sounds as though the peacock was killed mercifully, and the damage done afterwards. We did receive other similar reports from a couple of people who had brought birds to the Fotheringales and when they returned to check on their progress, they were told the birds had been killed by foxes. Others have said that they suspected they ended up on their table, but really this could be gossip. We have no reliable proof. I'm sorry to tell you this but we believe it's a good thing they've gone.'

'Someone brought us a duck only yesterday; she couldn't have known all this; she seemed to believe the Fotheringales were some sort of saints, rescuing birds.'

'Well, if you want to continue with your crusade, you had better let it be known that *you* are *not* the Fotheringales!'

That evening, she and Carl had a lot to discuss. First there was the cage to build and some fencing as well. Then there were security cameras to think about. Then Jenny said she would like to do a course on bird care, maybe with the RSPB. She could fit her telephone job around it. It would be wonderful, to be useful. The children they had hoped for had never come; this would fill a hole in her life she had never truly acknowledged was there.

She settled down with the computer to design leaflets, advertising, and looking into charity status for a business. She would turn it around: the unscrupulous behaviour that the Fotheringales had left. Smiling, she went outside and gave the geese some extra corn.

The next day, Jenny only had a few clients to contact and started her calls as soon as Carl had gone to work, but then the geese started up their chorus again. She knew not to ignore them now, so hastily went to investigate. The duck woman was waiting by the gate.

'Remember me?' she said, 'Becky, although I don't think we exchanged names before. Can I come in?'

'Of course. Actually, I'm glad you came, I have some questions.'

'Well, me too.'

Jenny told Becky about the peacock but reassured her the duck was fine.

'What did you want to ask me?'

'When I realised you weren't the Fotheringales, because I knew they were a lot older, I started asking around, and apparently, they were not as nice as I had been told. I mean, that was why I had brought the duck, and then, well, it was all right because you took

185

him in, anyway. But there was this one man who brought an owl for them to look after, but they didn't, they just let it go free and it was killed by crows. He found it in the next field when he was walking his dog. He confronted them, and they just lied about it.' Becky stopped to draw breath and Jenny took her opportunity.

'You think this man was vindictive? That he might have come back and killed the peacock? Sort of revenge?'

'Not sure about that, after all, he liked birds, didn't he? No. He also said Mrs F. had been visited by some protesters, the ones who break into laboratories that carry out experiments on animals, but maybe that wasn't the truth either.'

Jenny repeated all this to Carl, and they decided to put up the cameras straight away. They were pleased with the results: they worked well and they enjoyed watching the infra-red videos each morning and seeing the wildlife that visited the garden.

But then the duck went missing. He couldn't fly, so they were immediately worried and turned to the camera for some answers. To their horror, it showed a man creeping around the garden. They had heard nothing. The man was holding a sack or something similar and seemed to know his way about. Not a young man, they thought and Carl tried to get a close-up. Firstly, the man threw corn to the geese, keeping them busy and quiet, then he quickly bagged the duck. When Jenny saw this, with the camera so close, she threw out an arm to Carl as if to ward off the truth and drew a sharp intake of breath.

'That's Mr Fotheringale! He doesn't know about the cameras and he's stealing our duck! Do we confront him?' Jenny asked Carl.

'No, I don't expect he would turn violent or anything, but it's not worth the risk. We'll do the right thing and take this film to the police.'

'You're right. But they seemed to have some odd standards. I think Mr F. may have killed the peacock, you know, like a mercy killing, as she was so old. Then a fox came in afterwards. Or maybe the other way around. I don't think we shall ever know.'

186

The police were not sure what to make of the story Jenny and Carl told them, but they had received other similar complaints and were not too busy that day. They went to the Fotheringale's home that afternoon and were met by an enticing smell of roast duck.

DARKNESS   by S.F. Formi

The umbrella gave little or no shelter; three people were at least one or possibly two, too many. Katrine hunched her shoulders and tried to squeeze further away from the pelting rain. Greg was taking up most of the space; he should move away – his bulk was just too much. Her mouth turned down with resentment.

It had been early evening when they'd all arrived. The dying sun had provided a colourful backdrop over the city rooftops with red and gold bands streaking across the sky. But then the weather had changed and now the storm seemed to be set in for the night. Katrine's eyes strayed over the third member of the group: Alex's face was impassive. He never let his emotions show. She supposed that was how it had to be if you were a leader. After all you had to stay in control. She watched as the rain dripped down across the smooth forehead, ran down the straight nose and dripped off the end. Alex didn't move a muscle. Suddenly she wanted to laugh. Her mouth twitched with the effort of holding her mirth in. It was all so crazy.

Twenty minutes later the town was deserted, the distant sounds of the traffic began to fade away; the silence was oppressive, but then they heard the regular clip, clip of Margot's heels as she made her way towards them, her blonde hair hanging in rats' tails beneath the old-fashioned Homburg she always wore. Katrine saw Alex breathe out gently. He'd been worried Margot wasn't going to show! That must be it. Did that mean he didn't trust her? She was key to their arrangements. Katrine's keen eyes switched to Greg's face; searching his expression to see if he'd noticed anything. But Greg

188

was nodding a greeting to Margot and his countenance was bland and closed.

'What news?' said Alex, shifting slightly to make a space in the tight circle for her.

'He's there. My contact Gina told me he'll be there all night.'

'How can we be sure of that?' Katrine frowned. Margot showed a confidence in everything she said that sometimes irritated Katrine. Confidence of youth, she supposed.

Margot swung to face her, the folds of her trench coat shedding sparkles of rain.

Trench coat, thought Katrine. What with that and that hat, she's just a caricature.

'I've told you. Gina is perfectly reliable. She's not going to let us down.'

'Margot knows what she's doing.' Greg's eyes were now wide and intent and he started swaying from foot to foot as he spoke. 'She's checked the girl out and she has her own reasons. That's true, isn't it Margot?'

'It is. I've told you all. They destroyed her life she reckons, and she wants even.'

'Then,' said Greg, 'let's do it – now!' His face was alight, one hand curled into a fist thumped into the palm of the other.

'No,' the word was almost shouted and Margot's cheeks were flushed. 'We agreed. Not while the children are there. We must wait until tomorrow.'

'What!' roared Greg, 'he could be gone by then.'

'No, he won't. Gina got something to slip in his drink. She says he'll sleep late.'

'I say, now,' growled Greg.

'No.' Alex put his hand on Greg's shoulder. 'We'll do it the way we agreed. You'll keep tabs on her won't you Margot?'

'Of course.'

'Right,' said Alex, 'that pub's still open over there. We can run through it all and make sure we are ready for tomorrow.'

189

They sat by the fire, their outdoor clothes steaming gently in the warmth. Katrine looked at their faces, more relaxed now in the comforting ambience of the pub. She knew all their back stories; trafficking was an evil business; one they'd all had experience of in one way or another. She blinked and reached for a tissue as the image of her young sister came to her. Going over it all with Alex had been the hardest thing she'd done, but every bit of information was needed, Alex had said, if they were to succeed. She knew he was something in the Army, so that would account for a lot, she thought. She watched as he carried the drinks over to the table. Not a drop spilt. He was cool as a cucumber.

'So,' said Alex, 'let's just run through what we're each doing. Margot, your job is to keep the information coming in.'

Margot nodded. 'No problem.'

'Katrine, you are driving. Keep the car up the road a bit. '

'Greg?'

'I know what I'm doing.' He grinned and punched his hand hard several times.

Katrine cringed and looked at Margot, who was looking into the distance as if she wasn't there. They'd both wanted it to be a quick, clean finish.

'Right,' said Alex, 'and I'll go in with Greg.'

He reached for his glass and pushed it to the centre of the table. The others did the same until all the glasses were touching.

'Retribution,' he said.

'Retribution,' they repeated.

SOONER A LIVING COWARD   by S.F. Formi

Dear Rose,

I hope this finds you as it leaves me. I am not so bad, all things
considered. Of course, I could do with some of your delicious steak
and kidney pie! Won't that be a treat when I get home? How are the
little tinkers? Tell them Daddy misses them and we'll have fun
when I get home.
I can't say too much about where we are but just to let you know we
are on the road, so God willing, it won't be long.
Well dear, I would love to be with you, sitting by the fire and
making our plans but for now just remember to keep your pecker up
and think about the light at the end of the tunnel. It's not that far off
now.
All my love, Ron

The postcard fell into the room as the last piece of the old fireplace
came down. It was smudged and blotchy with soot and dirt, but the
writing was still legible. Laura stared at it, her eyes wide with
fascination. Where had this been sent from? When?

'Jules,' she called, 'come and look at this.'

'Hold on,' he said, 'just checking the paint, so we can get started
tomorrow.'

Jules arrived, his tee-shirt smeared with dust and paint, breathless
from the unaccustomed physical work.

'Here,' she said, handing him the postcard.

'Yeah, so...?' he said, scanning it quickly and turning it over.

'It must be pretty old,' she said. 'In fact,' she peered closer, 'I
wonder if it dates from the War, you know, World War II.'

'Why do you say that?'

'It's the tone – someone far away and longing to get home – and then that bit about not being able to say where he was...'

'Well, we'll never know. I should just bin it.'

'No. I'm going to talk to old Mr Williams next door.'

'Him! He's got to be about 110.'

'Exactly.'

Old Mr Williams had shaky hands, Laura noticed, as he took the postcard from her. Perhaps Jules was right; he was past it after all.

'Where d'you get this from Laura?' His voice trembled a bit too.

'We were taking out the old fireplace and it fell out. I wondered if you knew who Rose and Ron were?'

Bert Williams settled into his lumpy armchair with the sagging springs.

'Would you like a cuppa, love?' he said.

'No, no. I can't stop. I just wondered...'

'I could do with one. Would you mind putting the kettle on?'

'Well, yes of course.' Laura frowned and glanced at her watch, as she made her way to the kitchen, her nose wrinkling with the musty smell of damp. Perhaps it wasn't such a good idea, coming in here; there was so much to get on with indoors, but looking at that leaky radiator, they might have to give him a hand with the heating.

When she came back with the tea, Bert was sitting with a far-away look on his face. He's forgotten all about the postcard, she thought, but then he began, his voice high and whispery, but the words came clearly, without hesitation.

'Rose lived in that house, your house now, after she married and until she died. Of course, I've lived here, man and boy, so we were neighbours a long time.' He paused to take a sip of tea.

'But I was only a kid in the war and I didn't really know much about what had happened. Not until my Elsie died. We took the place on after my parents and we were very happy here. Not like you youngsters today – always looking for another house, bigger and better.' He gave her a sudden wicked grin.

192

Not much wrong with your brain, thought Laura.

'But then in 1960, Elsie got cancer. It was all over in a matter of months. And it was after that, Rose came to offer help and stayed for a chat.'

'So Ron was Rose's husband? What happened?'

'She'd had the telegram of course at the time but that doesn't tell you much. No, it was a mate of his from the Army. Came to see her. Told her.'

He fished a large white handkerchief from his cardigan pocket and wiped his eyes.

'Telling me started the tears off with her again.' He laughed, 'so there we both were, crying our eyes out over our respective losses.' He stopped again, and his face began working with long remembered emotion.

'This chap, Jim I think his name was, told Rose that Ron had taken him under his wing.' Bert nodded, 'Jim was just a young lad, shouldn't have been there really. Ron looked after him.'

He sighed and a moment passed.

'You know about Dunkirk, do you?' he peered at Laura.

'Yes, of course.'

'Well that's where it happened. Jim told Rose that he and Ron were waiting to get on one of the little ships. The beach was full of soldiers, all desperate to get on a boat. Get away from those Nazi planes that were mowing our boys down, strafing the beach, over and over.' His bony hand swept the room in a flattening movement.

Laura found herself rigid with tension. She thought she knew what was coming but had to hear it. She leaned forward

'So poor Ron was one of the unlucky ones?'

He looked at her a moment. 'The way Jim told it, Ron saved his life. When the Stuka came at them, he threw Jim to the ground and lay on top of him. Ron got it. Jim survived.'

A soft, 'Oh' escaped Laura. 'A hero,' she whispered.

'That didn't interest Rose. Remember, she was telling me this twenty years after the event, but she was still an angry woman.

'She said Jim talked about camaraderie in battle and Ron's gallant act and she had to stop herself from flying at him. "What use were heroic deeds to me?" she said to me, "he saved a boy and left his own children fatherless".'

A huge sigh left him. 'She never got over it. I've never forgotten what she said as she left me that day.

"I'd sooner a living coward by my side than a dead hero in the ground."

The old clock on the mantelpiece ticked into the silence in the room. Laura straightened up and took hold of Bert's hand. Stroking the thin, papery skin she said,

'Thank you for telling me.' She picked up the postcard and studied it a moment.

'I think I'm going to put this postcard into a frame and it will have pride of place in my house, in Rose's house.'

Bert smiled, his eyes misty with memories.

'It will be a sort of memorial to Ron and Rose – a reminder of what they both went through at that time,' she said.

'Lest we forget,' whispered Bert.

THE NEWCOMER   by S.F. Formi

Eliza lay in bed, her eyes wide open; sleep would not come. Eddie's whistling went on and on. She sighed and pulled the pillow over her head. *Who was he? This boy/man who'd just appeared in their family.* A long-lost cousin was Mother's explanation but why, wondered Eliza, had they never heard of him before?

Iris, of course, had been at her most girly: giggling and showing off constantly. She was too young to be bothered by the questions nagging at Eliza's brain. For Iris, Eddie's arrival had been a welcome break in the boredom of their lives, mostly spent closeted with their governess. The novelty of having someone young, and more particularly, of the opposite sex made Iris giddy with excitement.

But Eliza had been aware of a change in her mother's behaviour too. Usually so calm and controlled, she had become flustered and fumbled for words when she told them Eddie was coming. Eliza thought back to Eddie's arrival earlier that day. Iris had insisted on wearing her best dress and while they waited, had run backwards and forwards to the window in anticipation, her long blonde plaits bouncing on her shoulders.

Mother had spent the time pacing the floor, constantly pushing her straying curls back into place, her face unusually pale. Eliza herself had stood to one side: a grey shadow in her day dress. Since Miss Mortimer's departure for foreign climes, Eliza had been conscious, both of her status as the older sister and of Iris's need for a steadying influence, but then he had come, bursting through the door with the cold scent of the outdoors mingled with a musty male smell. Eliza had felt a flush rise in her cheeks and had been unable to control the quickening of her pulse. Everything the visitor had done increased Eliza's discomfort and Iris's wildness. He had insisted on playing a game and they'd all gone outdoors, wrapped in coats and bonnets. The game was tag. Faces flushed, the girls had run hither and thither until Iris's screams of delight began to border on hysteria and Mother stepped in to say tea was ready.

Eddie had sat down at table and seemed to have forgotten to wash his hands and also was unprepared for Grace. The girls watched as two cucumber sandwiches went into his mouth at once, which did not stop the constant stream of chatter and jokes. Scones, thickly spread with jam and cream, followed the sandwiches in short order. Wide-eyed with fascination at his unusual table manners, the girls forgot to eat themselves. Mother's sharp voice reminded them it was rude to stare, just as a chunk of fruit cake disappeared, crumbs tumbling down Eddie's shirt from the half-open mouth. It had all been so different from the way things usually were. Who was he?

Eliza jerked back to the present: there were two voices next door now. It seemed that Mother had entered Eddie's room. At first it was just a mumble, too low for Eliza to catch. Then a thump, as of someone stamping their foot, made her jump. Iris's eyes flew open.

'What was that? What's happening Eliza?'

'I don't know. I think Mother and Eddie are talking.'

'Talking,' Eliza realised, was not quite the right word, as the voices were becoming louder.

'How dare you speak to me like that?' Mother's tone was harsh and strident. Both girls sat up in bed, their bodies stiff and still as they strained to catch every word.

Eddie's response was muttered and indistinct. Then Mother again:

'Don't say that! It's a lie, a lie. You don't understand. How could you?'

Eddie's voice, louder now and with a snarl of fury, 'that's right. I was a child, wasn't I? I couldn't understand. And you hoped I'd never know, didn't you?'

196

The girls were frozen with shock. Was this smiling, whistling Eddie? Lithe and sunburnt Eddie with his cheap gaudy clothes, reminding them of a barrow boy but so much more exotic?

He had suddenly become something wild and angry. Iris shuffled closer to Eliza, then trembled as her mother's words came through.

'I did what I thought was right: the best I could. There was nothing else I could have done.' A soft moan followed. 'You should not have come. You don't belong here. Go, please go, and leave us in peace.'

Through the wall came a noise like a growl and then Eddie's words:

'I'll go, but not before I make sure everyone knows what you did. I'll spread your secret everywhere; you'll know what it's like to be the outsider.'

The girls had never heard such bitterness and for a moment there was stillness in both rooms. A heavy tread broke the tension and made the floorboards creak even louder than before. Eliza heard the squeak of the door hinges.

'He's going. It's all over. Thank goodness.' She closed her eyes and breathed a little easier.

But a sudden thud, a long slow groan, followed by a sliding sound, sent her nervous system into overdrive. Iris buried her face in her sister's shoulder. They clung to each other, shaking. There was nothing but the breath going quickly in and out of their own bodies.

Then began a slow dragging in the room next door. With this came a laboured breathing and the occasional grunt. Eliza recognised the click of the wardrobe door: then more grunting and gasping, and the sound of something being pushed and manipulated into place.

There was a deep, final grunt and then all was quiet. Slowly a soft keening began. Eliza felt the back of her neck begin to prickle as the sound reached her. Through the wall came a crooning.

'Eddie, Oh Eddie, beautiful Eddie. Why did you come? I'm sorry, so sorry.'

The girls clung to one another as if they'd never let go.

Dawn broke; the house stirred with morning noises; fires were laid by the maid; the smell and sizzle of breakfast drifted up the stairs.

A WINTER'S DREAM by S.F Formi

Though grey the morn, still snowdrops peep and gleam
through frozen land in winter's drear and gloom.
Frost stills the ripples in the icy stream
but I am snug and safe in my warm room.

Yet I dream on, yearning for summer days
that bring us laden boughs and meadows green
and skies so blue they pierce the morning's haze
while early birds sing and clucking hens preen.

Then streams of silver stars cross velvet nights.
But that's for then: now time to don our boots
and layered up, once or twice, maybe thrice,
we crunch and slip through fields where stark trees stand.

Eyebrows gain a frosty line, blur the view.
Homeward turn, while muscles burn, trudge through, trudge
through.

Printed by Amazon Italia Logistica S.r.l.
Torrazza Piemonte (TO), Italy

41625438R00112